A GANGSTA'S EMPIRE 2

**Lock Down Publications &
Ca$h Presents**
*A Gangsta's Empire 2
By Tranay Adams*

.

Lock Down Publications
P.O. Box 870494
Mesquite, Tx 75187

Visit our website at **www.lockdownpublications.com**

First Edition December 2018
Printed in the United States of America
This is a work of fiction. Names, characters, places, and incidents either are products of the author's imagination or are used fictitiously. Any similarity to actual events or locales or persons, living or dead, is entirely coincidental.

Cover design and layout by: Dynasty's Cover Me
Book interior design by: Shawn Walker
Edited by: Shon Progue

Stay Connected with Us!

Text **LOCKDOWN** to 22828 to stay up-to-date with new releases, sneak peaks, contests and more…

Thank you!

Submission Guideline.

Submit the first three chapters of your completed manuscript to ldpsubmissions@gmail.com, subject line: Your book's title. The manuscript must be in a .doc file and sent as an attachment. Document should be in Times New Roman, double spaced and in size 12 font. Also, provide your synopsis and full contact information. If sending multiple submissions, they must each be in a separate email.

Have a story but no way to send it electronically? You can still submit to LDP/Ca$h Presents. Send in the first three chapters, written or typed, of your completed manuscript to:

LDP: Submissions Dept
Po Box 870494
Mesquite, Tx 75187

DO NOT send original manuscript. Must be a duplicate.

Provide your synopsis and a cover letter containing your full contact information.

Thanks for considering LDP and Ca$h Presents.

CHAPTER ONE

Yada lie under her salmon pink silk sheets in bed, the side of her face pressed against her tear soaked pillow as she cried her eyes out in the dark. She couldn't believe that her father was murdered. And she couldn't wrap her head around the fact that it was her husband that had killed him. Yada didn't get it. How can someone that claimed to have loved her so much do something that they knew would hurt her so bad? She was in turmoil. Her heart ached, her soul was shattered, and her body felt weak. Yada wished she could squeeze her eyelids shut, and when she peeled them back open everything would be back to how it was when she'd woken up a week ago. A few times she did just that. But unfortunately, she found herself right where she was. Inside of her bedroom, with the lights out, crying her eyes out.

Knock, knock, knock, knock!

Rapping at the door stole Yada's attention from her grieving. She snatched a few tissues from out of the box of Kleenex sitting beside her canopy bed. Once she used them to dry her eyes and blew her nose, she balled them up and tossed them inside of the waste basket sitting at the side of her bed. Afterwards, she cleared her throat, and looked to the double doors of her master bedroom, responding to her visitor.

"Come in," Yada called out to whomever it was on the other side of the doors. A moment later one of the doors opened and Jabar's silhouette appeared.

"They found 'em, get dressed so we can go." Jabar said before shutting the door closed and walking out of the bedroom. With that having been said, Yada hopped out of bed and hurriedly got dressed so she could confront Voss, and put a bullet in his head for murking her old man. Five minutes flat and she was zipping up her jacket and ready to go. Before leaving, she picked up a portrait of her and her father, which was sitting on the nightstand beside the bed. As tears seeped from out of her eyes, a smile formed on her lips. She swallowed the spit in her throat, wiped her dripping eyes with the back of her hand and kissed the portrait. Once Yada sat the portrait back down on the night stand, she left her bedroom, pulling the door shut behind her.

***

Jabar pulled up outside of a white house with a gray rooftop. Its iron fence was scuffed with black marks, but its dying greenish brown lawn was manicured. The house wasn't much to look at. But upon first look you could tell that whomever its owner was kept the property and its surroundings tidy. Well, or at least they tried their best to.

"This is it, get out," Jabar instructed Yada before he jumped out of the car. He then kneeled down and pulled his banga from underneath the driver's seat. Once he recovered his piece, he slammed the driver's door shut and joined up with Yada who was patiently waiting for him on the curb. He nudged her and they entered the yard of the house he and the rest of Lyndell's goons called The House of Pain.

Jabar unlocked the front door of the house and held it open for Yada to enter. Once she did, he came in behind her. He pulled the door shut and locked it behind them. He then led Yada to the basement door, which had a key pad lock beside it, like a safe. Jabar lifted his finger to the key pad, allowing it to linger for a time as he tried to remember the code to it. He then punched in a combination of numbers and the door popped open. As soon as it did he could hear the grunts of a man as he pummeled someone who made pained noises. The sounds of fists pounding wet flesh made Jabar cringe. He knew it was Voss down in the basement and he was taking one hell of a beating.

The way the sound synced in when Jabar had opened the basement door, Yada knew the basement was soundproof. From where she was standing she could also see that the basement's concrete floor was stained burgundy which she assumed may have been blood that had settled and dried. Yada couldn't help wonder what kind of horror stories were behind those blood stains floors, and if the spirits of the dead haunted the house.

Jabar shut the iron door behind them and slid the huge iron latch across the door, securing it. He then tapped Yada and they made their way down the steps. Along the way they heard the barking of ferocious dogs and niggaz talking mad shit. When they reached the landing of the basement Yada was finally able to see what Voss looked like.

Voss's head was swollen to the size of a pumpkin, his right-eye was swollen shut, and his nose was broken. His face was bloody and sweaty. He was standing on the tips of his sneakers as his wrists were bound together by rope. The rope was hung over a wooden beam in the ceiling and tied to a radiator in the corner. Voss was a bloody mess. From the look of him he appeared to be knocking on death's door. He found himself wincing and wheezing with every breath that he took, feeling like his ribs were broken.

Bang and two goons were standing before Voss. They were all wearing black wife beaters, and their bodies were shiny from perspiration. The goons were holding Uzis as black as their clothing while Bang was warming up Voss's rib cage with punches.

"Ugh!" Voss's body jerked violently as Bang gave him one final punch to the midsection, causing him to spit up blood. The blood splattered on Bang's boot and the leg of his cargo pants. He looked down at the nasty glob angrily, then looked up at Voss with hatred in his eyes.

"Bitch ass nigga, you did that shit on purpose!" Bang gave him a three punch combination to the face. Voss's head swung to the left and then dropped down chin touching his chest.

"Woof! Woof! Woof! Woof!"

"Woof! Woof! Woof! Woof!"

The dogs, who were Rottweilers, barked louder and harder, saliva spraying from their mouths.

"Shut cho bitch ass up, nigga!" Bang got angry as fuck; he stormed over to one of the barking hounds and kicked the living shit out of it. The dog howled in pain and cowered in the corner of the basement. Seeing the dog being kicked, the other hound promptly shut the fuck up.

When Yada looked up at Voss and seen how fucked up he was, she couldn't stop the tears from spilling down her cheeks in buckets. She thought for sure she'd lost all of the love she had for him once she found out he was the one that had murdered her father. But seeing him in his current state brought all of her emotions rushing to the forefront for her. Her shoulders trembled like she was freezing cold and she brought her shaky hands to the lower half of her face.

Yada took a deep breath and blew out hot air, wiping her dripping eyes with her fingers. The noise she made caused Bang and the goons to look her way. The goons were about to spray her ass with their Uzis, until it registered to them who she was.

"Fuck you get here, nigga?" Bang asked Jabar as he approached and slapped hands with him.

"Just now. Y'all niggaz slipping, y'all didn't hear our asses come down here?" Jabar said as he looked up at battered and bruised Voss, dripping blood on the cement floor.

"Hell naw. When lil' mama made that noise my niggaz were about to start blasting."

"You straight, Yada?" Jabar asked her as he swept her hair from out of her face and caressed her cheek with the side of his hand, admiring her beautiful. Even when she was crying she was still attractive.

Yada wiped away more of her tears before answering him, saying, "I'll be—I'll be fine. It's just that seeing him brought back up what he'd done to my father. I mean, I—I really loved this nigga and he killed my daddy. Took him away from me," she sniffled and wiped her dripping nose with the back of her hand.

"That's okay, baby. I brought chu here tonight for some get back," Jabar assured her as he rubbed her back soothingly, keeping his eyes on Voss.

Yada turned to Jabar with furrowed brows, wondering what he was getting at. "Get back? Wha—what do you mean?"

Bang looked at Yada like she was retarded or some shit. "Well, damn, lil' mama, you sho is slow. I thought chu were born and bred in the slums."

"Nigga, fallback, she just lost her pops so she's not thinking straight," Jabar took up for Yada and then pulled a pair of black leather gloves from his back pocket, passing them to Yada. She looked at him like she didn't know what to do with them until he told her to put them on. She obliged. He then pulled his gun from the small of his back, holding it up and cocking a flat-head hollow tip bullet into its chamber. Using his gun, he motioned Yada over to him. He stood behind her and placed the gun into her hands, tilting the lethal end of it up toward Voss. "You ready to twist this nigga's cap back for slumping yo old man?"

Yada stared up at Voss with a tear soaked face, sniffling. She was feeling sorry for him, but then that sorrow turned into hatred. Again, her mind was bombarded by a barrage of the happiest moments of her and her father. Then finally the image of her father lying dead in her arms struck her mind like a bullet. Right then, her eyebrows arched, her nose crinkled and her jaws locked.

Fuck this nigga, Yada! Blast on his ass, he popped yo daddy, just like you said! Took him away from you forever. You can't let that shit slide! Do his punk ass; put a hot one right through his brain!

"Yeahhh, I'm ready," Yada told him confidently.

"Good." Jabar smiled devilishly.

Suddenly, Voss brought his head up. He looked up into Yada's face. His vision was blurry and he was seeing double. He blinked his eyelids a few times and tried his best to focus his sight. Finally, his vision came into focus, and he could clearly see Jabar standing behind Yada with a gun pointed up at him. He opened his mouth to say something and he winded up coughing up blood. He spat blood on the floor and cleared his throat as best he could to speak. He was still hoarse once he could finally say something, but he was sure Yada could hear him though.

"It—it—it wasn't me, baby. I—I didn't kill yo—yo pop—pops," Voss said with a hoarse voice, thick ropes of blood mixed with saliva hanging from his chin. "It was—it was Jabar. Jabar did it."

A furious Jabar came from behind Yada and pointed his finger at Voss, accusingly. "You lying ass bitch! I didn't kill 'em, you peeled the OG, and then shot me!

Took my mothafucking ear off!" Jar pointed to the thick bandage that lay over what was left of his war. "Ol' jealous ass mothafucka got mad at Lyndell 'cause he wanted you and me to split the responsibilities of second in command! Emotional ass bitch!" he looked him up and down like he was shit at the bottom of his sneaker, hating the sight of him.

"Fuck you, you fucking faggot! You're the one that's jealous! Jealous of what me and Yada have! Jealous that Lyndell took me under his wing and treated me like a son!" Voss looked at Yada. "Baby, listen to me, I put that on our love. I put that on our love that I didn't kill yo father!"

Blowl!

Voss slumped where he was hanging, his head bowed, leaving his chin touching his chest. Yada lowered the gun as it wafted with smoke, evaporating in the air.

"That's right, baby girl, handle yo mothafucking business." Jabar told Yada and then looked to Bang. "Check that bitch ass nigga's pulse and see if he's still breathing."

"Fa sho." Bang said as he approached Voss, placing two fingers on the side of his neck. His face frowned up. He looked over his shoulder at Jabar. "This ho ass nigga is still alive, man!"

"Hard to fucking kill," Jabar said under his breath and turned to Yada. "Baby girl, gon' put one in that nigga head, get this shit over with so I can have my niggaz dispose of his body."

"Nah," Yada shook her head, eyes still on Voss, watching his chest slowly rise and fall, as he took short breaths.

"What chu mean, nah? This nigga popped yo goddamn daddy! It's only right that chu get cho revenge for it." Jabar reasoned.

"Fuck this nigga!" Yada spat on the floor and looked back up at Voss. "I want his ass to hang there and bleed to death."

"You mean let 'em suffer?" Jabar asked.

"You goddamn right."

Jabar smiled devilishly and said, "I respect yo gangsta, slim, for real for real." He took the gun away from Yada and stuck it back into the small of his back. "Alright, you got it. We gon' let this bitch nigga bleed to death then we gon' get rid of the body."

Jabar turned to Bang and the goons, telling them what to do with Voss's body once he was officially dead. He then tapped Yada and they made their way toward the staircase. Yada's eyes lingered on Voss. Hot tears stung her eyes and water ran down her cheeks. She then mouthed 'I love you'. With that having been soundlessly said, she turned back around and headed up the staircase.

"Listen, I'ma kick it at cho crib. I don't think it's a good idea that chu be alone tonight." Jabar told Yada from behind the wheel. The street light flickered on and off of them through the windshield, taking them in and out of darkness.

"Oh, you don't have to do that. I'll be fine." Yada assured him.

"Nah. I'ma take care of you. I know that's what OG would want me to do. And I don't mind."

"Well, if you insist." Yada focused her attention out of the passenger window, watching the street fly past her.

***

When Yada and Jabar came through the door of her mansion, she heard a noise that stole her attention. Her brows crinkled and she looked at Jabar, who was rubbing his stomach.

"Nigga, you farted?" Yada asked seriously covering her nose and mouth.

"Nah, that was my stomach growling. I'm hungrier than a bitch. You think you can hooka nigga up witta sandwich or something?" Jabar inquired as he walked towards the living room.

"Yeah, just limme use the bathroom right quick. Make yo self at home." She watched Jabar flop down on the living room couch and grab the remote control, flipping on the television set.

Yada headed upstairs where she raised the commode's lid, pretending to take a piss. She then turned on the faucet water, allowing the water to flow as she searched the medicine cabinet for a bottle of Benadryl. She took the capsules down and stashed them inside of her pocket. She then cut the water off and headed back down stairs, passing by Jabar as she headed inside of the kitchen. Jabar licked his lips and grabbed the bulge in his jeans watching her bodacious ass bounce from left to right. He then focused his eyes back on the flat screen TV.

"What kinda sandwich do you want?" Yada asked right before she disappeared through the doorway.

"Salami, please," he responded, "Extra mayo, lettuce, pickles, onions and tomatoes, oh, and mustard."

Yada went inside of the refrigerator and took out all of the items she'd need to prepare Jabar a salami sandwich. She then grabbed the loaf of bread from out of the pantry. As she went along with making Jabar's sandwich, she called out to him.

"Aye, what do ya want to drink?" Yada's voice rang out inside of the living room."A Heineken, if you got one." Jabar responded.

"Hold up," she held the refrigerator door open as she looked through the shelves, finding the beer he desired. "Yeah, we got Heineken."

"Cool." She heard him respond.

Yada finished making the sandwich and sucked the mayo off of her thumb. She put the items she'd used away, and grabbed the Heineken. She took the bottle-opener out of the kitchen drawer and popped the top on it. She then looked back and forth between the bottle of beer and the kitchen door, opening the Benadryl capsules and dumping their contents inside of the bottle. Once she was done, she discarded the capsules and placed the sandwich on a plate along with a few cheese and cheddar potato chips. Picking the plate up, Yada made her way inside of the living room where she saw Jabar on his cellular, its screen shining on his face.

"Dinner is served," Yada entered the room with a smile on her face, sitting the plate and beer down on the coffee table before him.

"Thank you," Jabar sat his cell phone down and pigged out on the food. Yada watched him stuff his face for a moment before she left the room. She returned an hour later to find Jabar's ugly ass slumped on the couch, snoring like a mothafucka, with his mouth wide open.

"Sleeping Beauty," Yada said before she headed back upstairs, and inside of her bedroom. She strapped on a Kevlar bulletproof vest, threw on a hoodie, gloves, tied a black bandana around her neck and grabbed her .45 automatic handgun from underneath the mattress. Gripping it with both hands, she pointed it at something imaginary across the bedroom, taking aim. Satisfied with her gun of choice, she tucked it into the small of her back. She then grabbed her cell phone and dialed up LeLe who was out doing God only knows what, telling her where to meet her. Once she disconnected the call, she made her way out of the mansion and into the night where she jumped inside of the passenger seat of Dough Boy's car.

Tranay Adams

CHAPTER TWO

Bang and the goons kicked it on the front porch of The House of Pain, waiting for that nigga Voss to die off. They shot the shit while passing a smoldering blunt between them. Bang had just hit the bleezy and passed it to one of the goons, when his cellular suddenly rung. Reaching into his pocket, he pulled it out and looked at its screen. B.M. was on the display.

"Shit!" Bang said staring at the cell phone's screen, blowing smoke out of his nostrils and mouth.

"What's up, bro?" one of the goons asked holding smoke in his lungs before blowing it out in a cloud.

"It's my baby momma. I was supposed to slide out with her crazy ass to her mother's birthday party. I know this bitch ain't doing nothing but calling to cuss my ass out, and I don't feel like hearing that shit. I already know she gon' keep banging my line until I pick it up though so I may as well face the fucking music. Y'all niggaz be quiet for a second, man."

"Alright." The goon responded before passing the blunt to the other.

"'Sup?" Bang spoke into the cellular. His brows furrowed and his eyes shifted back and forth as he listened to what was being told to him. "Junior? How the fuck did that happen? Shiiiit. What hospital they taking 'em to? Ok. I'll see you up there." He disconnected the call and turned to the goons. "Look, y'all, I gotta go. Some shit came up with my son. Once that nigga down there is dead, y'all get rid of the body." Bang ran from off the porch, hopped the fence with one hand over to the sidewalk and ran across the street. He opened the door to his Charger, hopped in behind the wheel, and peeled off. The wheels of his tires screeched as he busted a U-turn in the middle of the street and sped off in the opposite direction.

"Yo, you think that nigga baby momma really called 'em, or was he front so he could get outta helpin' us get rid of homeboy's body?" the goon said, cupping his hand around the half smoked blunt hanging from his mouth and lighting it again. He sucked on the end of the blunt and blew out a cloud of smoke.

"Somebody called 'em, but I doubt it was about his fucking kid. I'm witchu. That nigga just didn't wanna help us with this goddamn body. Sorry ass motha—" the goon was cut short when his dome suddenly exploded, and his brain splattered against the house. He fell over the banister and landed hard on his back with a thud.

When the other goon saw his homeboy fall over the banister, his eyes grew big and he looked around for where the bullet had come from. He couldn't identify where the shot was fired from so he reached for the newspaper, which was covering his Uzi. He'd just snatched the newspaper from off his weapon, when the side of his skull exploded. His brain fragments went up in the air and rained down to the floor. The goon's body hit the surface, and right after came his blunt with its ember burning.

As soon as the last goon was laid out dead, there was ruffling in the bushes on either side of the house. Suddenly, Dough Boy arose from the left bushes, gloved hand holding a Glock with a silencer on its barrel. His menacing eyes were peering out of the holes of a burgundy ski mask. He made his way up the steps and onto the porch. He moved to each goon, kicking them in their side and watching them, to see if they'd move. They stayed still. At that moment, Yada emerged with a .45 automatic handgun with a silencer on its barrel. She was wearing a blue bandana over her head and over the lower half of her mouth. Her eyes were hidden behind black sunglasses.

She'd taken out the second goon while that nigga Dough Boy had laid down the first goon.

Yada motioned for Dough Boy to follow her as she opened the front door of the house. She moved inside of the house like a police officer, swaying her .45 from left to right. Once she figured out the upstairs was clear, she moved toward the basement door.

"Stand back, I got this!" Dough Boy told her, and went to aim his Glock at the key pad's lock. He thought he was going to fire a shot at the goddamn thing and it was going to short circuit. That way the iron door would open, and they could make their way inside. The nigga watched way too many movies!

"Hold up!" Yada outstretched her hand and motioned for him to lower his gun. "I think I remember the code for it," She looked at the floor, looking like she was in deep thought. Once she figured that she had recalled the combination that Jabar had punched in, she stepped to the key pad and punched in the number. The door beeped and flashed red. The combination was wrong. She tried again. Still didn't work. "Fuck, fuck, fuck!"

"Come on now! We gotta go! There are two dead bodies outside. Ain't no telling who seen what, and are going to blow the whistle to The Ones." Dough Boy told her. He was looking over his shoulder every five seconds, impatiently bouncing from foot to foot.

"Hold the fuck on!" Yada kept her eyes cast to the floor as she tried to recall the code again. Figuring that she remembered the combination that Jabar had entered, Yada punched in the number. The door beeped and flashed green. The iron door popped open.

Yada pulled open the door. Holding her gun with both hands, she crept down the staircase, carefully. Dough Boy was right behind her, gripping his shit up with both hands, creeping down the steps just like she was. When they made it down to the landing of the basement, they saw the Rottweilers licking Voss's blood up from the cement floor. Yada moved in, swaying her .45 from left to right, nozzle spitting flames. The dogs yelped painfully and fell out dead, holes in their skulls.

"We're here, baby! Me and Dough Boy! Hold on; we're gonna get chu outta here!" Yada tucked her warm gun into the small of her back and pulled the blue bandana down from the lower half of her face. "Dough Boy, you grab 'em, I'ma cut 'em down." She told her counterpart and unsheathed the bowie knife from her side. As she approached the end of the rope to cut her man down, Dough Boy looked around the basement until he found a blanket. He flapped it out and made his way toward Voss.

Yada waited by the radiator with the knife in her hand. Once she saw that Dough Boy was prepared to grab Voss before he hit the floor, she chopped the rope twice. The rope gave on the second swing, and Dough Boy caught Voss before he could hit the cement floor, covering him up with the blanket. The first thing he did was look at the gunshot wound in Voss's torso, which was on the right side, away from his vital organs.

"Good, good. You didn't hit anything that would have killed him instantly." Dough Boy announced to Yada. She walked over to them and placed her fingers on his neck, checking his pulse. Voss's eyes were rolled into the back of his head and his mouth was slightly peeled open. He was moaning, and in great pain, but he was still alive.

"Thank God. We've gotta hurry up so you can get 'em to the hospital. Come on." Yada pulled the blue bandana back up over the lower half of her face and pulled out her .45. She made her way back up the staircase, gun leading the way, and Dough Boy on her heels carrying Voss.

Yada and Dough Boy made hurried footsteps out of the yard and down the sidewalk, heading toward Dough Boy's Easter Bunny white Denali. Yada tucked her gun at the small of her back and pulled open the passenger door. She moved aside and let Dough Boy sit Voss down in the seat. He then ran over to the driver's door and jumped in behind the wheel, slamming the door shut behind him.

Yada pressed her finger against the ear bud in her ear and spoke. "Le, pull up, we're at Dough Boy's truck." At that moment, LeLe sped up the block and stopped, tires screeching. Yada peered over the windshield of the Denali. She held up one finger, signaling for LeLe to give her one minute. She wanted a moment with Voss before he was driven away.

"Baby, baby, baby," Yada called for Voss's attention but he didn't answer. He moaned and groaned. That's when she cupped his face and looked into his eyes. His pupil was moving around aimlessly, and he was still moaning. "Baby, focus, look at me," She sniffled, tears threatening to spill from out of her eyes.

Voss' eyes focused on Yada's tear streaked face. "Yada, is that—is that really you, baby?" He asked weakly. His left eye was swollen shut. He could see through his right eye, but his vision was tinted red from blood running into it. He continuously blinked it trying to keep more blood from getting into it.

"Oh, yes, yes, baby, it's me!" she sniffled again and tears slowly spilled down her cheeks. "Oh, my God, Voss, I love you. I love you so much, baby."

"Why—why did you shoot me, then?"

"I'm sorry, baby. I'm so, so sorry. But I had to in order to get Jabar to believe I wanted you dead. But everything is going to be ok, 'cause Dough Boy is going to see to it that chu get to the hospital. Ok?"

"O—okay."

"Baby, listen, I'm going to ask you something, and I need to know the truth. Can you do that? Can you tell me the truth, no matter what it is?" he nodded yes. "Baby, did you...did you kill my father?" Yada watched to see if his right-eye would twitch when he answered. But he didn't say anything and his eye didn't move. He was too busy moaning in pain.

"Hos—hospital," Voss croaked, wincing.

"Look, ma, that's a question better asked at another time. Right now, I need to get 'em to a hospital, ASAP."

"Ok." Yada nodded rapidly. She wiped her teardrops away. "Dough Boy is going to take you to the hospital now. You hang on, you just hang on 'til you get there and get some help." She kissed him tenderly on the lips. She then turned to the passenger window, fogging it up with her hot breath. A fresh set of tears pooled in her eyes, obscuring her vision. Using her finger, she wrote *I Love You.* Voss watched as the fog cleared up and the words disappeared.

Yada kissed Voss again. She then slammed the door shut behind her, and ran over to LeLe car. She jumped into the passenger seat and slammed the door shut. As soon as she did, LeLe pulled off heading into another direction while Dough Boy went in the other.

"Is Voss going to be ok?" LeLe asked, glancing back and forth between the windshield and Yada.

"I don't know…God I don't know. But I hope so 'cause if not, I'll die. I know I'll die 'cause it will be all my fault." Yada's voice became shaky and cracked under her raw emotions. She broke down, slobbering and crying, hands pressed against her face. Yada didn't know for sure if Voss was going to make it to the hospital on time or not but she was going to beg and plead with God to spare his life, even if it meant taking hers so that he could live. Little mama had already lost her mother and father, so if she was to lose the only man she'd ever truly loved, she'd go insane. Her heart would shatter into a million pieces, and her soul would quake. The loss of Voss Jordan would definitely be a loss that she could not take.

LeLe glanced back and forth between the windshield and Yada. She then pulled Yada under her arm, hugging her against the side of her body. "Shhhhh, shhhhh, everything is going to be all right, momma. Voss is going to make it to the hospital. You just watch and see. God's got 'em." LeLe kissed the top of Yada's head as she continued to rub her arm, sympathetically. Yada continued to cry her eyes out, as they drove along.

***

Dough Boy looked back and forth between the windshield and Voss, making sure he was still breathing.

"You good, my nigga?" Dough Boy questioned with concern.

"Yea—yeah, I'll be fine," Voss said, with his attention focused out of the passenger window. He was thinking about the note Yada left behind. "Roll the windows up and turn the heat on for me," He told him weakly. Dough Boy rolled up the window is his truck, and cut on the heater. A minute later the note that Yada had written on the passenger window appeared, I Love You. A slight smirk formed on Voss's lips as he stared at the message. Dough Boy glanced over at him to see what he'd had in mind to do. He watched as he wrote with his finger, too. As in *I Love You, Too.* He then envisioned Yada's face before his eyes, smiling at him as she stared at him admiringly. He smiled back at her.

***

LeLe pulled up in the driveway of Yada's mansion and slaughtered the engine.

Yada turned to LeLe and said, "Thanks for always having my back, girl."

LeLe waved her off like it wasn't a big deal and countered. "Don't even mention it, girl. You know you my nigga, and I'd do anything for you. And vice versa. You know how we do."

"You my bitch forever," Yada said, swearing her allegiance to their friendship.

"Forever and a day, momma," She hugged Yada affectionately, and kissed her on the cheek.

The girls then hopped out of the car. LeLe went on up the steps while Yada pulled her hood down over her head and tucked her hands inside of her hoodie, walking up the steps behind her. Pulling out her keys, Yada pressed her ear against the front door and listened closely. Little mama felt like she'd given Jabar enough Benadryl, to put him out for a while. But she could never be too sure. When she didn't hear anything besides the television playing inside of the living room, she unlocked the door and she and LeLe stepped inside. Yada shut the door behind them quietly, locking it. The girls hugged one another once again, before LeLe made her departure upstairs.

Yada turned her attention to the living room.

She could see the top of Jabar's head standing where she was, at the door. From the way he was slumped on the couch, she knew his ass was asleep. Placing her keys inside of her pocket, she slowly walked inside of the living room. Coming upon Jabar, she saw that he was indeed asleep. His glass of juice was empty and sitting on the coffee table next to his plate of half eaten tuna sandwich. Homie was snoring aloud. He suddenly made an ugly face, dug in his nose and then farted.

"I don't know if you killed my daddy or not. But if I find out you did, that's gon' be yo ass, nigga." Yada scowled. She then made her hand into the shape of a gun and pointed it at Jabar, pretending to shoot him dead. The light from the flat screen television danced across the upper half of her body. Her eyes lingered on him for a moment longer, before she made her way upstairs to her bedroom.

***

Boom!

The double doors of the emergency ward flew open. The hospital staff rushed Voss along on a gurney, tearing open his shirt and exposing the black bleeding hole in his torso. His eyes were hooded, and his pupils moved around lazily. He tried to say something and winded up coughing up blood.

"Hold on, my nigga, Hold on!" a teary eyed Dough Boy told Voss, running alongside the gurney, clutching his hand. Dough Boy tried to maintain his G, but seeing his homie all fucked up like that caused the tears to fall and drench his face. Once they started it was like he couldn't stop them from falling.

"Sir, I'm going to need you to let him go. We'll take care of him from here," one of the doctors told Dough Boy. The big homie wasn't trying to hear him though. His main concern was the condition that his right-hand man was in.

Voss's eyes became glassy with tears as he stared up at the ceiling. He could see angels in all white flying back and forth across the ceiling, playing violins and smiling at him, flapping their long feathery wings. They were shining brightly and had an eerie mystique to them. Voss didn't know what it was but them being there brought a sense of comfort to him. As funny as it may seem, giving his current circumstances, their presence made him feel as if everything was going to be fine.

Dough Boy's face balled up, because it seemed as if Voss was looking at something. He looked where Voss's line of vision ended and didn't find anything there. Then, that's when it came to Dough Boy that he was probably looking up at an angel or a deceased loved one.

"Nah, Blood, you can't go with them! You gotta stay here with us! Stay here with us, dawg!" Dough Boy urged him, tears bursting out of his eyes. Dough Boy pulled a burgundy bandana from out of his right back pocket and tied it around Voss's right wrist. Voss didn't take his eyes off the angels flying in circles above his head. A smile spread across his lips, and tears of joy spilled down his cheeks.

"I'm sorry, sir, but you've gotta go. We've gotta do our job," the doctor that had spoken to Dough Boy earlier said, pulling his hand free from Voss' hand. Slowly, Dough Boy's palm and fingers released his hand. Right then, another doctor looped an oxygen mask over his nose and mouth. Inside of the mask fogged with each weak breath that he took, lungs inflating and deflating.

Standing where she was inside of the hallway, Dough Boy saluted Voss with the Blood gang sign.

"Stay strong, Blood! Stay strong!"

Dough Boy's words echoed throughout the hallway as he stood where he was, watching the hospital staff rush Voss into emergency surgery. Standing where he was inside of the corridor, Dough Boy watched the gurney and the hospital staff become as small as ants before his eyes.

***

Jabar lie slumped on the couch still fast asleep. The sun's rays shined through the window and kissed off of his face. There was knocking at the door which grew louder and louder the longer it took for someone to answer it.

"I'm coming!" Yada called out as she reached the front door, coming from downstairs.

Knock, knock, knock, knock!

"I said 'hold the fuck on!" Yada called out again. The knocking stopped as she reached the door. She peered out of the window, recognizing who it was at her front door. Her brows furrowed with surprise. She then went on and unlocked the door, pulling it open. As soon as she pulled the door back, Bang walked inside of her house with a couple of goons bringing up the rear. He had a dead serious expression on his face and didn't bother to speak, which Yada felt was rude, considering he was entering her home.

"Well, hello, to you too, Bang," Yada tightened her robe on her and shut the front door, locking it back. Once she did, she entered the living room along with everyone else to see what was going on.

"Yo, wake up, wake up!" Bang called out to Jabar, but he wasn't waking up. "I said 'wake yo punk ass up, nigga!" he kicked the hell out of the couch which finally woke Jabar up.

A frowning Jabar stirred awake looking at Bang like he was crazy. He actually had the thought of picking up his gun, which was lying on the side of him beneath a pillow and shooting his mothafucking ass for breaking his sleep. The only reason why he didn't was because he figured if he was there then it had to have been very important. He had told the nigga where he was at and to hit him up if he needed him, but he'd decided to drop by instead.

Jabar sat up on the couch, stretching his arms and yawning, looking around at all of the goons surrounding him. All of them niggaz were wearing dead serious expressions and looked like they were ready to bring it to niggaz that violated. That's exactly why that nigga Lyndell had them on his payroll. They were a bunch of head hunting niggaz from different hoods all over Southern California.

"Fuck you want? Can't chu see I was getting my beauty sleep?" Jabar picked up his pack of Newports, taking out a cigarette and sparking it up. He tossed the pack back on the table, sucked on the end of the square and blew out a big ass cloud of smoke. He then scratched his temple with his thumb, giving Bang his undivided attention.

"Jerome and Titty are dead! Niggaz hit the spot and snatched up Voss!" Bang informed him regretfully.

"What the fuck you mean?" Jabar frowned up and shot to his feet, blowing smoke from his nose and mouth. "If they dead, how the fuck is yo black ass still alive?"

Bang explained to Jabar the emergency that came up that called for his immediate attention. With the report having been given to him, Jabar nodded, understanding the urgency.

"This shit was an inside job. All the niggaz that knew where we were taking that nigga were in-house." Jabar told him.

"You bet cho nut sack it is, and we're about to find out who did it, too." Bang assured him.

"How?" Jabar's forehead creased with curiosity.

Bang twisted his lips and shook his head, looking at Jabar like he was an imbecile. "The surveillance cameras we had installed you forgetful mothafucka! I got the tape right here." He held up the VHS tape to the surveillance cameras.

Yada's eyes widened when she saw Bang hold up the video tape. She sunk further in the background, moving toward the front door. She took a step back and bumped into someone. She turned around and found one of the goons behind her. When she looked around, she noticed she was surrounded by goons. Them niggaz had her closed in, and there wasn't any way she could get out.

"Excuse me," Yada said to the goon, but he didn't say shit back. She turned back around and stuck her hand inside of her robe, gripping her gun. If shit went left then she was going to blast her way up out that bitch!

Jabar smiled evilly and took the tape from Bang, saying, "Whoever in this room busted homie outta that house is a dead man! I don't give a fuck who it is! Bang, guard the door, I'ma 'bouta put the tape in." With that having been said, Jabar approached the DVD/VHS player to put the tape in.

Bang brushed pasted Yada, pulling out his banga so he could stand guard at the front door. Yada glanced over her shoulder and he did just that. When she turned back around Jabar was popping the surveillance tape into the VCR. The footage showed her and Dough Boy storming the house that Voss was being held hostage in, entering the basement and taking out the Rottweilers. It then showed her about to pull the blue bandana down from her face to reveal her identity. At that moment everybody in the living room, including Jabar, pulled out their guns to execute the traitor.

Oh, shit!

Yada thought as she swallowed the lump of fear in her throat and gripped her gun tighter. She knew then that *that* day may very well be her last day breathing.

Suddenly, static filled the television screen.

"What the fuck happened?" Jabar said, grabbing the remote to VCR/DVD player. He rewound and fast forwarded the tape but all it showed was static every time it went back to Yada pulling the bandana down to reveal her identity. "Aw, this is some ol' bullshit, dawg! Yo, Bang, Bang!"

"What's up?" Bang answered from the front door.

"Fucks up with this tape, nigga?"

Bang watched as Jabar rewound and fast forward the tape to the part where Yada was about to reveal her identity, each time he did the flat screen filled with static.

"Limme see it," Bang took the remote control from him and tried himself. He got the same results. "This shit fucked up, man. It's gotta be cause of these old ass tapes. I told yo ass we shoulda bought a surveillance system that exported into DVDs."

"Fuck!" Jabar snatched off his baseball cap and threw it on the floor, stomping it out, cussing up a storm.

"fuck, fuck, fuck, fuck! Now, how are we 'pose to find out who the fuck busted this fool outta The House of Pain?"

"The truth always comes to the light, dawg," A mad dogging Bang said as he looked over all of the goons, hoping one of them would expose themselves as the traitor. "Best believe that."

Jabar paced the floor running his hand down his face and exhaling. His nostrils flared and he took a deep breath. He was on one. The nigga was hotter than fish grease. Suddenly, he stopped pacing the floor and turned to the goons. "Alright, man, everyone besides Tankhead and Bang get the fuck from outta here, now!" With his command given, the goons left his house. Yada sighed with relief and took her hand out of the pocket of her robe, releasing her .45 automatic handgun. She thought she was going to have to shoot her way up out of that bitch, but through the grace of God she made it through the ordeal unscathed.

"Aye, you need me for something? 'Cause if not I was gonna go take a shower." Yada told Jabar.

"Nah, ma, you good. Gone 'head 'bout cha business."

"Okay." Yada said. She went upstairs to her bedroom and got some undergarments. Afterwards, she ducked off inside of the bathroom and shut the door behind her.

CHAPTER THREE

Yada entered the bathroom and closed the door shut behind her. She hung her robe on the hook on the back of the door, and walked over to the porcelain sink. She put toothpaste on her toothbrush and turned on the faucet water. Having wet her toothbrush, she went about the task of brushing her teeth. Once she was done, she rinsed off her toothbrush and placed it inside of the cup holder. Afterwards, she turned the dials on and the shower nozzle sprayed water. She adjusted the temperature of the spraying liquid to her liking, and then began to remove her bra. She had just slipped one of the straps of her bra off when someone entered the bathroom. Her brows furrowed, and she turned around, placing her bra strap back on her shoulder. She was surprised to find Bang behind her smiling wickedly.

"Excuse me, but I'm sure you know how to knock," Yada told him. She was visibly pissed off.

"Yeah, I know how to knock; I just didn't feel like it." Bang admitted.

"Well, you needa mind yo manners in my fucking house, homeboy, I'm not dressed."

"That's okay," he got close enough to kiss her on the lips, sliding his hands up and down her arms, and admiring her shapely body. He always wanted to tap that ass, but didn't know if she'd give him the time of day. "You being half naked means you're almost prepared for what I'm about to propose," he stuck his tongue out of his mouth and licked the side of her face, leaving a wet streak behind. Yada's face frowned up and her bottom lip turned downward, making the 'ewwww' look. She shoved his ass backwards, nearly causing him to fall, but he caught his balance.

"Keep yo dick tuggers off of me, nigga! For you to even insinuate that I'd even fuck the likes of you makes my pussy as dry as the fucking Saharah." She wiped the side of her face with the back of her fist.

"Oh, really?" he stepped closer to her. In fact, he was so close that she could smell his breath. It was kind of funky since he hadn't brushed his teeth that morning. He'd gotten a call from one of the goons saying that Voss had been busted out of The House of Pain and he shot his ass right over there. The nigga didn't bother to brush his teeth or wash his funky ass.

"Really." A frowned up Yada told him.

Bang smiled and brought his lips to her left ear, whispering in it. "Well, what if I told you that I have another copy of that tape I gave Jabar, and on that one it shows your face clearly. Would that convince you to give up that pussy?" he grabbed her by her pussy and she smacked his hand down. He then brought his fingertips to his nose and shut his eyelids, inhaling her scent. He made a face like she smelled of the best fragrance.

Look at this sick perverted mothafucka! Yada thought to herself, looking at Bang in disgust.

"Tell me, sweet cheeks, would that change your mind?"

Yada stood there mad dogging Bang and clenching her jaws, making them pulsate. She had no intentions on fucking Bang's slimy ass, no matter what kind of evidence he had on her. She wasn't going to come right out and say it though. You see, she needed some time to formulate some kind of plan to get herself out of her situation. So, somehow she had to lead this mothafucka to believe that she'd consider fucking him.

"Do you really have another tape that shows my face?" she asked timidly and afraid.

"I sure do, beloved," Bang swept her hair from out of her face and tucked it behind her ear, circling her face with his curled finger.

"Can…can you gimme some time to think about it?"

With that having been said, Bang whispered into Yada's left ear, saying, "Sure. I'll give you some time to think it over, but don't keep me waiting too long." When Bang turned around to walk away, he found a mad dogging LeLe at the door with a meat cleaver and a butcher's knife. "And what the fuck do you plan on doing with those?" he asked seriously. The smile disappeared from his face once he saw LeLe with those cooking utensils.

"A whole lot if you put cho hands on my girl, bitch!" LeLe swore, following him out of the door with her evil eyes.

"Everybody's a gangsta these days. Boy, I'll tell ya." Bang shook his head and left the bathroom.

LeLe sat the meat cleaver and butcher's knife down on the commode. She then shut the bathroom door and locked it behind her. When she turned back around, she found Yada hunched over the sink, trembling. She rushed over to her and gave her a hug. Yada became teary eyed. That encounter with Bang had her shook. Although little mama was strong, she was still a female. She thought she was about to get raped. If it led to that she wasn't going down without a fight. She would have gotten to her robe as fast as she could and emptied an entire clip into Bang's bitch ass for trying to violate her.

"Everything is going to be okay. Alright, ma, I'm here now. I got chu." LeLe said to her in a hushed tone, rubbing her hand up and down her bestie's back.

"Nigga had me shook, sis. I don't know what the fuck was about to happen." Yada admitted to her fear.

She took a couple of deep breaths and calmed herself down as best as she could.

"Me either, girl. I overheard the conversation downstairs, and I thought they were about start in on you. I didn't trust shit since that nigga Jabar been holed up here so I kept that cleaver and that butcher's knife under my pillow just in case shit crack off."

"Thanks for looking out." Yada said to her.

"Please, you know you my bitch." LeLe dapped her up. "Look, you want me to hole up in here while you take yo shower?"

"Nah, I think I'll be all right." She told her as she took her gun out of her robe, checking the magazine of her banga. She already knew it was fully loaded, but she checked it out of habit anyway.

Yada placed her gun in the corner of the shower. This way, if Bang or someone else tried some shit she was going to blow their fucking brains out of their head.

"My girl stays strapped." LeLe smiled proudly. She wasn't a scary bitch, but Yada was definitely more 'bout it than she was.

"Please, believe me."

"Okay. I'ma lay back down for a minute. I'm supposed to hang with Maul. Anyway, if shit jump off in here, shout me a holla and I'll come running."

"Okay."

"I love you." LeLe gave her a hug.

"I love you too." Yada responded.

Afterwards, LeLe stuck her meat cleaver and butcher's knife inside of her robe and left the bathroom.

***

Once Yada had finished showering and brushing her teeth, she took her robe off the back of the door and slipped it on, tying it around her waist. She then opened the door and stepped out of the bathroom, heading to her bedroom. Along the way she overheard Jabar talking to Bang and Tankhead.

"I want chu two niggaz to hit them May Mays tonight." Jabar told his top goons. "It's time to let that cocksucka Valdez know that the old man is gon' and I'm the new regime. We ain't sharing our mothafucking corners with nobody! Fuck that! I want it all! I want chu to leave one of them rice and bean eating mothafuckaz alive to tell the tale, but that's it. Everyone else getting some hot shit. Capeesh?" he looked from Bang to Tankhead.

"Yeah. I got chu." Bang smiled and bit down on his bottom lip, rubbing his hands together evilly. He couldn't wait to get in the middle of some shit. The nigga lived to beef with mothafuckaz.

"We'll take care of it, G." Tankhead assured Jabar. Jabar dapped up his top goons, and they dispersed.

Yada went inside of her bedroom and got dressed for the day. She planned on making a few runs before she went to see Voss in the hospital. Having slipped on her jean jacket and thrown the strap of her purse over her shoulder, she came out of her bedroom. Yada went down the staircase and headed for the door. She'd pulled the door open, when she heard someone going through the cabinets. Curious about whom it was, she headed inside of the kitchen where she found Jabar rifling through the cupboards. She asked him what he was looking for which startled him. He turned around to her looking shook as a mothafucka and whipping his gun out.

"Girl, you scared the fuck outta my ass!" Jabar admitted with a scared look written across his face and his banga out at his side.

"My bad. What're you looking for?" Yada asked, with wonderment on her face.

"Y'all ain't got no Henn Dog or Jack in this mothafucka?" he asked as he tucked his gun on his waistline.

"Yeah, limme get it for you." She sat her purse down on the island and grabbed a chair from the table, sitting it up against the refrigerator. She stood upon the seat of the chair and opened the cupboard above the refrigerator, taking down a bottle of Hennessy. The entire time she was getting down the bottle, Jabar's ugly ass was admiring her form lustfully. "Here you go." Yada passed the bottle to Jabar and he set it on the island to help her down. She put the chair back where she'd gotten it from, and turned back around. She watched him load his glass with ice cubes and pour his glass half full with Hennessy.

Jabar took a sip of the alcohol and brought his glass down from his lips, wiping his mouth with the back of his fist. He continued to drink as he stared at Yada, thoughts running through his mind.

"I've been meaning to ask you, that night that we almost, uh, that night that we almost got it in."

"What about it?"

"Was it happening 'cause you were drunk and vulnerable, or 'cause you wanted it to happen?"

Yada took the time to think about what Jabar had just asked her before answering. She knew what kind of situation she was in and that it was best to have him on her side. Especially with Bang having that fucking video tape hanging over her head. She noted that Jabar wanted her in the worse way, and she could use that against him for her survival. So she knew it was best to play like she wanted him just as bad as he wanted her.

"I was drunk and I was vulnerable, but I wanted it. But I saw Voss staring at me through my reflection in the mirror and it ruined the mood for me. I guess all that weed and alcohol got to me."

Jabar nodded his understanding and said, "I feel you. How come you never fucked with a nigga like that? I mean, I know I'm not the handsomest nigga, but I make up for it in other places."

Yada took a deep breath before responding. "I'ma keep it a buck witchu, a bitch wasn't fucking witchu like that 'cause I felt like all you wanted to do was hit it and quit it. And I made that assumption when I saw all of those hoodrat ass bitchez I see you flaunting all around town. Plus, all you ever do is tell yo homies about this and that hoe you done popped off."

"I'll admit to it. A nigga was out here being a straight up hoe, but I was gon' change the game when it came to you. I put that on everything, ma. I felt like you were the one." He held his left hand up to God solemnly swearing.

"I feel you. But niggaz out here be running game so you never know what's real."

"Do you ever think about us being together?"

"Of course. But I know I'm not quite ready yet 'cause I still haven't gotten over what lil' feelings I have for Voss. Yeah, he did murder my daddy, but feelings don't die overnight. You understand that, don't chu?"

He nodded and said, "I love you. I've loved you since, like, forever. And I don't expect you to say it back 'cause I know you don't feel like that. At least not now you don't, but one day in the future, I hope you will."

"One day in the future. I know I will." She caressed the side of his face and kissed him on the cheek. She then grabbed her purse from off the island and walked out of the kitchen, hips swinging from side to side. Jabar watched her until she disappeared through the kitchen's doorway and then sipped his glass of Hennessy.

***

Dough Boy paced the visiting room floor waiting for the doctor to tell him what was going on with Voss. When he finally arrived he told him that he was finally out of surgery and they'd successfully gotten the bullet out of him. He was stabilized but unfortunately he was in a coma. He also told him that it was up to Voss if he was going to come out of the coma and go on to live a fulfilled life. When Dough Boy asked could he see Voss, the doctor granted him permission to go see him. With the okay given, Dough Boy made his way down the hallway towards his comrade's room. Stopping at his door, he took the time to gather himself. He shut his eyelids and took a deep breath.

Dough turned the knob and pushed the door of Voss's room open as quietly as a cat burglar. When he stuck his head inside of the room, he found his best friend lying up in bed with his arms at his sides. He had tubes in his nose and an IV in his arm. His head was still swollen and he had cuts and bruises all over his face. There were also bandages wrapped around his torso which blood was slowly beginning to stain. Voss was hooked up to all kinds of machinery to keep him alive and breathing. The noise the medical equipment made was the only sounds inside of his dimly lit room. Voss was teetering between life and death, but by the expression on his face one would have sworn he was asleep.

Damn, Voss Blood, look at what them fuck-niggaz did to you, homie! I swear on my daddy's grave we gon' get them niggaz once you heal up. I don't care how much power that bitch ass nigga Jabar got. He and his people gon' have to see me and my guns, Dough Boy thought to himself as he pulled a chair up to his best friend's bedside.

As he shook his head thinking about his right-hand man's ordeal, wetness accumulated in his eyes and his bottom lip trembled. A whimper escaped his lips as he watched Voss fight for his life, his chest slowly rising and falling. He was in bad shape, real bad shape. Dough Boy couldn't stop the tears from falling from his eyes, but as soon as they fell he wiped his eyes with the lower half of his shirt, sniffling. Feeling snot threatening to drip from his nose, Dough Boy snatched a few Kleenexes from the box sitting beside Voss's bed and used them to blow and wipe his nose. He then balled the tissues up and tossed them inside of the wastebasket. Having licked his lips and cleared his throat with his fist to his mouth. He placed Voss's hand within his own hand and grasped it, holding it affectionately.

That night, in the room with death looming over his best friend's head, a gangsta cried.

That night

"What's the science behind these niggaz who caps Jabar want us to peel back, man?" Tankhead asked Bang from behind the wheel of the G-ride. He was a short, big head, black ass nigga who rocked his hair in short corn-rows. He was wearing a beanie and a long sleeve black T-shirt beneath a Kevlar bulletproof vest.

"These Mexican fools are a part of the BDOG; Jabar wants us to hit 'em." Bang informed him as he loaded up them thangz and click clacked them. He was wearing a wave cap, black T-shirt, which was underneath a Kevlar bulletproof vest, and a black bandana that was around his neck like a cowboy. "This is his way of sending 'em a message. His way of letting these bean eating niggaz know, we're not settling for a slice no more. Nahhhh, we want the whole mothafucking pie."

"Say no more, my nigga. Hand me that shotty from off of the backseat, dawg." Tankhead told him. Bang grabbed the shotgun and racked it, passing it along to him. Tankhead laid the shotgun on his lap and pulled over across the street from a liquor store that closed at the moment. There was a few Mexican men kicking it out front, selling drugs to the occasional junkie that walked up on them.

"That's them?" Tankhead asked, staring out of the driver's window.

"Yeah, most def. The tall one with the ponytail is rocking a leather vest with BDOG and that stupid fucking cartoon dog on it." Bang pointed with his finger. "Call 'em over here, Doe."

"Alright," Tankhead whistled at the dude in the leather vest, motioning for him to come across the street. He turned around and pointed a thumb at his chest. "Yeah, I'm tryna get right."

The Mexican in the leather vest jogged across the street, looking both ways for any oncoming cars. He stopped for a second to let a Toyota pickup truck pass him, before continuing across the street. As soon as the Mexican man in the leather vest came upon the window, Tankhead pointed his shotgun at his face. His eyes got big and he gasped. His head disintegrated as the barrel of the shotgun erupted. His lifeless body collapsed into the street, and Tankhead threw open the driver's door, hopping out. He and Bang ran across the street, seeing the Mexicans scatter in every direction. They said fuck it and started blasting recklessly, figuring they'd hit someone, and they did. Bodies were dropping from left to right. Their victims lay on the sidewalk and halfway off the curb, bleeding. Their blood soiled the concrete burgundy and left it wet, dripping into the gutter.

Tankhead and Bang looked to their right, up the block, seeing a Mexican with his hair cut in a fade. He was holding his bleeding ass and limping away, occasionally glancing over his shoulder to see if the men that represented a threat to his life was on his ass or not. Tankhead reloaded the shotgun. He was about to blow a hole through his monkey ass, but Bang raised his gun and told him to fall back. He then tucked one of his guns on his waistline. He then charged at the limping Mexican and jumped up into the air, kicking him in his upper back. The Mexican fool hit the ground hard, wincing.

"Turn yo bitch ass over, nigga!" Bang ordered him, pointing his gun at his head. Slowly, the Mexican man turned over, locking eyes with Bang.

"If you gon' kill me then kill me, foo! I ain't afraid to die!" the Mexican man egged him on. If Bang thought he was going to plead for his life then he had him fucked up. Just like he lived his life as a gangsta, he would die as one as well.

"I'm not gon' kill yo wet back ass! You're gonna be my lil' message boy." Bang pressed the hot barrel of his steel into the Mexican man's cheek causing it to sizzle and burn his flesh. Once he pulled his gun back, there was a small bloody, black circle left behind. "I want chu to tell Valdez that Lyndell is dead and Jabar is running the show now. The truce is over, and we want these corners back. And if we don't get 'em back then we knocking off the heads of any Mexican we see in these streets, comprende, ese?"

"I got it!" the Mexican winced.

"Good. You can have the rest of this clip for your troubles." Bang pointed his gun at the Mexican nigga'z legs, pumping them full of holes.

Blocka, blocka, blocka, blocka, blocka, blocka!

"Aaahhhh! Aaaahhhh!" The Mexican man hollered out in agony and lay back on the sidewalk, holding both of his bloody, bleeding legs.

Meanwhile, Tankhead and Bang ran across the street, looking both ways for any oncoming cars. They jumped inside of the G-ride and peeled off from the scene.

CHAPTER FOUR

The Mexican man that Bang had left alive, Johnny, was lying up in the hospital with the lights out in his room. He was wearing a hospital issued gown and boxers. He was lying on his stomach to keep pressure off of the gunshot wound in his ass, and both of his legs wore casts. There were autographs from his friends and family on the casts in a variety of colors. His little cousins had drawn houses, their family, dogs and hearts on it. While his girlfriend had placed her name and an imprint kiss which left her red lipstick behind.

Having eaten, gotten a sponge bath and enjoyed his time with visitors, Johnny lay asleep in bed, facing the window. Feeling a presence inside of his room, his eyelids snapped up and he sucked up the drool that dripped from the corner of his mouth. His eyes shots to their corners, hearing the footfalls of his approaching visitor and the chair that he grabbed on the way over to the side he was facing.

The man sat the chair down beside Johnny's bed. He sat down, crossed his legs and removed his black sunglasses, tucking them inside of his shirt's breast pocket. He then adjusted himself in his seat, causing the chain hanging from his jean pocket to rattle a little. "Johnny, how're you doing?"

"I'm out of it, homes. I'm doped up on morphine." Johnny told him in a groggily voice. Once his vision came into focus from his sleeping, he could tell that his visitor had been crying. He could make out his face through the small rays of light shining in through the enormous window, coming from the windows of the opposite window. His visitor's eyes were pink and glassy. He also had dried white lines on his face from his tears drying on his cheeks. "I'm—I'm sorry about jour cousin, mano. I truly am. He was my—my best friend, and I'm going to miss 'em, dearly." He found his eyes building with tears and he blinked them back as best as he could, but they eventually dripped from the brims of his eyes anyway. "What's the big man saying?"

The visitor found his self crying again so he whipped his bandana from out of his back pocket and dried his eyes, sniffling. He then tucked the bandana back into his back pocket. "Valdez is pissed, homie. He wants ol' boy executed on sight. He was going to fly out someone to handle the job, but I requested the assignment specifically. This one is personal. It got that way once they assassinated my cousin; you know what I'm saying?"

Johnny nodded his head as more tears accumulated in his eyes, saying, "I feel you. You get 'em, get 'em for Bandit, aye."

"I will. I swear on his life," he slipped on his black sunglasses, uncrossed his legs and stood to his feet. He patted Johnny on his shoulder affectionately and told him he'd be back to see him soon, before heading for the door.

***

Yada visited Voss at the hospital; she brought him a dozen of the most beautiful roses she'd ever seen and a card. She'd also brought along an iPod she'd bought for him. She downloaded all of the songs she knew he loved as well as some songs she wanted him to listen to.

Yada filled a clear burgundy vase with water and placed the roses inside of it, sitting it on the windowpane. She then sat the card she'd bought on the windowpane beside it. Afterwards, Yada walked over to

Voss and kissed him on his dry, ashy lips and caressed his forehead with her hand. She cracked a smile thinking about his smile and the good times that they had.

"Hey, my love, I had a long talk with Treasure last night. She told me about her late fiancé getting shot up in a botched hit. Anyway, he found himself lying up in the hospital, life teetering between life and death, unable to come out of a coma until she played this song. The song I'm about to play you, right now. Once she played this song, her man seemed to come back to life, and he got well, he got better. I'm hoping—"

Yada bowed her head as her voice cracked with her emotions and tears threatened to fall from her eyes. She sniffled and looked back up, wiping her dripping eyes with her thumbs and fingers. "I'm hoping that this song she recorded, way back then, Unstoppable, will somehow do the same for you." She took a deep breath, and pulled out the iPod she'd bought for Voss. She placed the earphones inside of Voss's ears. Her thumb went through the device until she found the track that Treasure believed helped her then fiancé, Pain, out of his coma. Once Yada came upon the song, she pressed *play* and stuck it into Voss's partially opened hand. She cranked the volume on the iPod and looked up at Voss, watching for any reaction to the song. Yada ran her hand up and down her husband's tattooed arm affectionately. She paid close attention to Voss's facial features as the music played in his ears—

This willpower, this spirit, it's too solid
They can't break it
I won't stop I can't stop, I'm built for this. I'ma make it
I will live, I will talk, I will walk. I'm dedicated
I will live, I will talk, I will walk. I'm dedicated.

I'm unstttttopppablllllle, they say I won't but I'ma talk agaiiiin

I'm unstttttopppablllllle, they say I won't but I'ma walk agaiiiin

I'm unstttttopppablllllle, I'ma do it alllllllllll agaiiiiin

I'm unstttttopppablllllle, there's no way that I cannot wiiiiiiiiiiiin

Seeing a flicker of movement at the corner of her eye, Yada looked over her shoulder but she didn't see anything. At first she thought she'd seen something fly across the enormous window, but she chalked it up to her mind playing tricks on her. Pushing the thought to the back of her head, Yada focused her attention back on Voss, still running her hand up and down his arm. She saw the flicker of movement again out the corner of her eye again, but this time, she didn't turn around. Nah, she waited a moment, and then, her head snapped in that direction. Tears welled up in her eyes and her lips quivered, as she smacked her hands over her mouth.

Outside the window, Yada saw crows flapping around, causing their feathers to float around in the air. The crows continued to fly around, making 'caw' sounds over and over again, making more of their feathers swim around in the air. The crows signified Death to Yada. Her grandmother told her when she was a little girl that a crow stood at your door, window, and car or anywhere around you that death was sure to come shortly thereafter. And every time Yada encountered the black bird, there it was—*death!*

"Get away, get away, you goddamn birds!" Yada picked up the pitcher of water that was sitting on the rolling table top, and slung it at the window. The pitcher exploded, and water splashed everywhere but the birds continued to hang outside of the window. Acknowledging this, Yada picked up the chair she was sitting in and flung it at the window. The chair deflected off of the window's glass, and fell on the floor, on its side. "Get away, get away! Get the fuck away from his window! I love him, I love him and you can't have 'em, goddamn it! You hear me? You can't fucking have 'em!" she removed her shoes and threw them at the window, one by one. The shoes deflected off the window, but the god damn birds kept flying around outside of the window.

Just then, the door swung open and Dough Boy rushed inside. His forehead was crinkled and he was looking around the room at what could have possibly been going on for Yada to have been behaving the way she was.

"Yada, what's going on? What happened?" Dough Boy inquired as he approached.

"These birds, Dough Boy! These birds symbolize death!" Yada claimed continuing smacking the glass window and yelling at the crow, trying to get them to fly away. The birds weren't going anywhere though.

"Hey, what's going on in here?" a voice rang out from behind them. They looked over their shoulder and found a security guard and a nurse standing at the door.

"Look, Yada, maybe you should—" Dough Boy was cut short once the heart monitor sounded off, and Voss started convulsing in his bed.

"Shit, he's convulsing!" the nurse called out and ran over to Voss. She called out to the security guard, telling him to get Dough Boy and Yada out of Voss's room.

"See, it's happening! I told you, I told you! They want him," Yada made an ugly face as she looked on at the love of her life, shaking and rocking in bed. She couldn't help wondering would today be the last time she'd see him alive, as the security guard ushered her and Dough Boy out of his room.

Dough Boy and Yada was ushered out of Voss's room, just as the medical staff poured inside of his room to attend to him. Out in the hallway, Dough Boy held Yada in his arms as she cried her eyes out, hoping that Voss pulled through and came back into their lives.

The next day

Yada strolled through the tall double doors of the church, which had ceilings as high as the clouds in the sky. God's house was dimly lit with the sunlight shining through the opened doors and the colorful, stained-glass windows with religious figures on them. The pews were made of dark brown wood with padded, burgundy cushioning on the seats and backrest. The carpet was flat and charcoal gray. A matching rug ran from the entrance of the church to the stage where the podium resided.

Stopping before the enormous gray crucifix, Yada got down on her knees before it and put her hands together in prayer. Lowering her head, tears burst from her eyes and slid down her cheeks. The tears dripped from her chin and splashed on the carpeted floor. She sniffled before she began her conversation with the crucifix.

"God, I come to you today to ask that you spare Voss Jordan, the love of my life. Lord, if you were to take him from me, at this time in my life, I just know my heart couldn't take it. My heart, my soul, my body would all crack and shatter into pieces. After the murder of my daddy, I cannot begin to fathom the emotional hurt I'd experience. I seriously believe that I wouldn't recover from another loss. I know you know that I am strong but there's only so much that one person can take." And with that, Yada fell apart, sobbing and crying while holding on to the bottom half of the crucifix. After a while, she quieted down and held her position there at the lower half of the statue. Next, she cleared her throat and wiped her eyes and nose with Kleenex from out of her purse. Getting up from off her knees, she headed for the exit of the church and disappeared through its doors.

Seven days later

A week had passed since the doctors had gotten Voss stabilized. He'd given Dough Boy and Yada one hell of a scare. They'd thought for sure that he was on his way out, but the Lord was merciful, he gave Voss another chance, one that his loved ones took advantage of.

Yada had to leave the day that Voss went into shock. The last thing she wanted was Jabar getting suspicious of her going missing for long periods of time she couldn't account for. She knew then that he'd connect the dots and figure out that she was the one that had busted Voss out of The House of Pain and was probably disappearing from time to time to check in on him. She'd be in a lose, lose situation then. And she couldn't have that.

Dough Boy found himself at his best friend's bed-side, head bowed and fingers interlocked. Yada had suggested that he let Voss listen to his iPod while he was laid up in a coma. So he did. He didn't know the story behind Treasure's late fiancé coming out of his coma after listening to Unstoppable, so it was a coinci-dence, when the song started playing in Voss's ear-phones. Dough Boy took a deep breath and brought his face up, sliding his hands down his face. He looked to Voss's face, seeing his eyelids twitching. He looked to his feet, and his toes were beginning to move. Unstop-pable continued to play in his earphones—

I'm unstttttopppablllllle, they say I won't but I'ma talk agaiiiin

I'm unstttttopppablllllle, they say I won't but I'ma walk agaiiiin

I'm unstttttopppablllllle, I'ma do it alllllllllll agaiiiin

I'm unstttttopppablllllle, there's no way that I cannot wiiiiiiiiiiin

"Holy shit, my nigga's moving! He's fucking moving!"

Dough Boy hopped to his feet and darted out of the room, his burgundy Nike Cortez sneakers screeching on the floor. He ran down the corridor, stealing everyone's attention that he came across, his reflection shown on the waxed floor as he hauled ass down the hallway. Dough Boy came across the doctor that was taking care of Voss and pulled him back towards his room.

***

Ding!

The elevator stopped on the fourteenth floor and the door opened. Yada made her way adjusting her purse on her shoulder. She rounded the corner and made her way down the hallway, nodding to the hospital staff and visitors she came across. Looking up ahead, she saw Dough Boy and Voss emerging from his room. Dough Boy was holding him up under his arm while he walked down the hallway, pushing an IV pole. A smile spread across Yada's face and she speedwalked towards them, calling out to him.

"Baby, is that you?" Yada called out to him.

Voss looked up, forehead creasing, saying, "Yada? Baby, is that you down there?" he started speed walking towards her too. In fact, he was moving pretty fast because he'd gotten away from Dough Boy and was moving on his own, pushing the IV pole along with him.

"Yes, it's me!" Voss said, jogging down the hallway as fast as he could, his reflection shown on the floor. The hospital staff and visitors that were around him were looking at him and Yada wondering what was going on.

"Oh, my God, it is you!" Yada said aloud, her eyes instantly filling with tears. Before she knew it, buckets of tears were pouring down her cheeks. She slung her purse to the floor and took off running in her lover's direction, her hair and jacket ruffled in the wind. The visitors that were walking in her direction moved out of her way for fear of being knocked down.

"It is you, babe." Voss said aloud, tears building in his eyes. He jogged faster after her, holding the area of his body he'd been shot at. It was numb from the morphine the nurse had given him, so his holding it was more out of habit than anything else.

Yada and Voss met each other halfway before she jumped into his arms. She wrapped her arms around his shoulders and her legs around his waist. They fell to the floor slowly, with him still being weak and unable to support her weight. Yada found herself on top of him, cupping his face and staring into his eyes.

"It's you, it's really you, babe! I can't believe it, I can't believe my eyes." Yada cried more and more, staring into the face of the man she knew she was destined to spend the rest of her life with. "I thought—I thought I'd lost you forever. Oh, my God, I love you, babe. I love you so much, I don't know what I'd do if I ever lost you. You're all I've ever been able to think about, boo. I couldn't function without chu being here by my side." She planted what looked like a million kisses all over his face, pausing for a moment to kiss him on his lips.

"I thought I lost you too, ma. I thought I'd never ever seen you again. I thought God was gon' let me die for all the shit I did out here in these streets, but he didn't; he allowed me to live. I had to beg 'em, but I thank 'em for giving me another shot, because I had to see you again, ma. I had to hold you, I had to kiss you and look you in yo eyes and tell you I love you. And that you're the greatest thing to have ever happened to a nigga like me. You're my rib, my heart, my soul, my everything, and I don't ever want to lose you again." Voss's voice broke under his emotions and he found himself crying like a baby. He tried to hold it in like the gangsta that he was but he couldn't. His emotions had become too much for him and they cracked his exterior armor, and exposed his true feelings.

The Jordan's' broke down hard crying and then kissing. Once they stopped making out, they cupped one another's faces and held their foreheads against one another's. They stared into each other's eyes, and smiles formed across their lips. They were so happy to see one another alive again. That neither one of them wanted to let the other go for fear that they'd lose the other.

Dough Boy and the rest of the hospital staff wore jovial expressions on their faces as they watched the exchange between Voss and Yada.

Voss and Yada wiped the tears from one another's eyes with their thumbs. Yada then sniffled and said, "Babe, I don't mean to ruin the moment, but I've gotta ask you this. And I need for you to be completely honest with me, okay?"

"Ask me whatever you wanna ask me, sweetheart. And I'll tell you no lies." Voss swore to her, holding her gaze.

"Okay," Yada took the time to clear her throat before continuing. "The night at your welcome home party, were you the one that killed my daddy?"

Voss continued to hold her gaze as he said, "Yada, I swear on our love to wither and die, that I did not murder your father. That nigga Jabar shot him then turned the gun on his self. He was trying to shoot himself in the shoulder, but the dumb mothafucka blew half of his ear off. I solemnly swear that *that* is the honest to God trust. I hope you believe me."

Yada bowed her head as he continued to hold her face cupped in his hands. He kissed her all over her face, just like she'd done him when they first met in the hallway. Tears continuously streamed down Yada's cheeks, dripping off her chin.

"I believe you, babe. Now, there's something I've gotta tell you. I hope it doesn't change the way you look at me, and you stop loving me for it," She looked up into his eyes, hoping he wasn't already looking at her sideway, but he wasn't. He was looking at her curiously, wondering what she had to tell him that could possibly change the way he viewed her.

"Spit it out, kid. Whatever it is, we'll deal with it." He swore to her then kissed her on the forehead.

Yada took a breath that made her shoulders slump. She then went on to tell Voss that she'd almost had sex with Jabar, watching his face for a reaction. He didn't bat an eyelash when she revealed the news to him. He nodded his head and said, "I'm not wetting it. You were hurt and confused. You'd just lost yo pops, and you thought that I betrayed you. Your actions are understandable, especially under the influence of alcohol."

"Thank you for understanding. And I swear on our love that something like that will never ever happen again." Yada vowed to him. He nodded and kissed her again.

"Come on, y'all. We're drawing a crowd out in this hall. Let's go back to the room," Dough Boy extended his hand. Yada took his hand and he pulled her to her feet. While he busied himself helping Voss up, she jogged down the hallway and recovered her purse, gathering the few items that spilled from out of it. Afterwards, she jogged back to the room where Dough Boy and Voss had gone. She found Dough Boy helping Voss sit down on the edge of his bed, and rolling his IV pole aside. The fat man then walked around the bed and sat down in the big chair in the far corner, right beside the enormous glass window.

When Voss looked to the door and saw Yada, he motioned her over to him and patted the empty space on the bed beside him. Walking over to him, Yada sat her purse down on the push table's top and sat down beside her husband, interlocking her fingers with his.

"I know that nigga'z keeping a close eye on you, so where'd you tell 'em you were going?" Voss inquired.

"I told 'em I was running to the store and picking up some dry cleaning." Yada informed him.

"You sure you weren't tailed here, ma?"

"Yeah, I'm sure. I made sure no one was following me, and I switched up cars at a parking garage, just to throw niggaz off in case they were on me. Shit, I do that shit every time I come down here to see you. I'm not stupid. Plus, you know yo girl packing. I treat my foe-five like American Express; I never leave home without it." When she said this, Voss smiled broadly, liking the fact he had a chick on his arm that was street smart and knew how to handle herself. He'd dealt with square chicks before in the past, and they definitely weren't suited to be on his arm.

"That's my girl." He kissed her on the cheek. "Fill me in on what's been popping since I've been out of the mix." Once Yada finished filling Voss in on everything that had occurred since he'd been laid up inside of the hospital, he stared ahead and massaged his chin, thinking deeply. "If he's really running the show like you said he is, then I can't go up against him. At least not now. That nigga has more funds, guns and soldiers than I do. He'd squash me like a fucking cockroach."

"I've been thinking, babe," Yada sat up on the bed. "He's sweet on me. So I can get right up under his ass. I can wait 'til he lets his guard down and slit his shit from ear to ear." She said with a dead serious expression etched across her face, pretending to cut her throat with an imaginary knife.

"Nah," he shook his head as he laid his hand on her thigh. "If you take him out, them other fools will fa sho knock yo head off. You see, they respect me and him 'cause we been in the fields putting in mad work for the organization. Although you have gotten yo hands dirty in the past, they don't know about that 'cause they weren't there. To them dudes, it's not what chu did then but what the fuck you doing now. You feel what I'm saying?" she nodded. "As soon as you'd pop 'em they'd be popping you. And I can't have that. If that happened, I'd show them fuck-boys a level of savagery they'd never seen before."

"Then what do you suggest we do?" Dough Boy spoke up for the first time. He'd been so tired that they'd forgotten that he was even present.

"I'ma have to get my mind, my body and my money right if I'm gonna lock ass with this fool. Ain't no ifs, ands or buts about it. I cannot see 'em unless I got plenty of paypa and soldiers." Voss assured him.

"You remember my relatives I was telling you about down in Vegas earlier?" Dough Boy inquired. Voss nodded. "Well, they fucked up down here. They don't got a plug with decent drugs so business has slowed to a crawl. I was thinking we could cop us a couple of bricks and go down there to make shit move and shake. The shits an open market. We can get rich damn near over-night from what he tells me about how many smokers they got down there."

"What cho peoples moving, P?" Voss asked him from over his shoulder. He and Yada's attention was now focused on Dough Boy.

"They're moving that *boy* down there."

"Heroin," Voss massaged his chin as he was think-ing deeply again. "I gotta plug on some dog food I met while I was locked up. I saved his ass and he promised to hook me up on some dope anytime I decided to get in the game. I guess it's time I cashed in on that favor."

"You're gonna need money, babe." Yada told him.

"She's right. I'm sitting on about twenty-five grand. I know it ain't much, but I'm willing to kick it all in for the cause." Dough Boy said sincerely. Voss was his main man, fifty grand, and he'd follow him into the depth of hell busting his gun to kill the devil, if he'd asked him to. The best friends were just that loyal to one another.

"That's why I love you, Dough. You always hadda nigga'z back no matter what the situation was. Respect." He gave him a complex gang handshake.

"Right back at chu, P."

"Hold on to that though, my nigga. I got us cov-ered." He looked at Yada and said, "I need you to get me a million dollars of that money you put up for me. You think you can do that?"

Yada thought on it for a second and then said, "Yeah. The bank is gonna wanna know what the hell I want with all that money at once. But I know a couple of strings I can pull to get it outta there without them getting too suspicious."

"Thanks, ma."

"You're welcome, lover." She kissed him.

"I'ma also need you to pack me a bag of clothes, shoes, my bulletproof vest and guns. I'll meet up witchu in like two days."

"Two days? If you just woke up outta that coma then these people aren't going to let chu go."

"They will. Trust me." He told her. "I just gotta sign a form that says I'm releasing them of all liability is all."

"Okay."

"Good. I'ma hit cho line from Dough Boy's jack, just in case Jabar's around and see whose calling you. Alright?"

"Alright," she nodded.

Seeing that his boo was a little worried, Voss caressed the side of her face and looked in her eyes. "Ma, I need you right now, okay? I needa know that chu got this. So, tell me. You look me right in my eyes and tell me, bae, don't worry about nothing. I love you, I got this. Can you do that for me, lover, huh? Can you?"

Yada cleared her throat and looked her man square in his eyes, saying. "Bae, don't worry about nothing. I love you, I got this." They then kissed.

"Alright then. That's what I like to here." He said. "One more thing."

"What's that?" her brows creased wondering what else he could want from her.

"You do any and everything you have to do to keep that nigga'z suspicions to a minimum, even if it means fucking 'em. We're on a mission. And we've gotta do

61

what we've gotta do for our cause. Don't mind me tripping off what chu do with 'em cause after this is all over. We starting over again and we're never gonna talk about this again. You got me?"

"I got *us*." She told him, seriousness dripping from her eyes.

With her response, he kissed her on the mouth again, lovingly.

Two nights later

Dough Boy pulled into the Target on Redondo Beach and parked in the back, away from all of the other patrons' vehicles. He and Voss scanned the parking lot looking for Yada's vehicle, but they didn't see it. Voss glanced at the digital clock on the dashboard, and looked back up, taking an impatient breath. Having grown tired of waiting, he pulled out his cellular phone and was about to hit up Yada, when Dough Boy nudged him and pointed to her car, through the windshield. Yada pulled into the row of parking spaces that they were on and parked directly across from them. Once she killed her engine and hopped out, Voss hopped out and made his way over to her. She was just raising the trunk of her car when he'd reached her. She grabbed the duffle bag from out of the trunk and gave it to him. He sat the duffle bag on the opening of the trunk and unzipped it, taking a gander at everything inside.

"That bag has the million dollars in cash you requested, the guns and the bulletproof vest." Yada told him as she stared at the duffle bag he'd peered inside of. She then looked to the other duffle bag inside of the trunk. "The other bag has all of your under garments and hygiene products."

"Okay." Voss said, zipping up the duffle bag and looping its strap over his shoulders. He then grabbed the other duffle bag and looped its strap over his shoulders. For a minute he stood there, staring into Yada's eyes, not knowing what quite to say to her. She stared right back at him, only she had a million and one things to say to him. And not enough time to say it all.

Suddenly, Yada hugged him and shut her eyelids tightly, tears sliding down her cheeks. She then kissed him on his lips like she hadn't seen him in years. When she pulled back, he caressed her cheek with the side of his hand.

"You really love a nigga, huh?" Voss asked, staring into her eyes.

Yada nodded yes and said, "They haven't created the words to express how much I love you, Voss. It really doesn't make any sense how far gone I am over you." She grasped his wrist and kissed the inside of his palm tenderly.

"Dido."

"I prayed, babe. I prayed and prayed and prayed, and then I prayed some more for you to come back to me," She said sincerely. Tears slid down her cheeks and he wiped them away with his thumps as he cupped her beautiful face, looking upon her like she was more precious than gold. "I was afraid. I was afraid that I'd never see the only man I ever loved in this entire world again. The thought of that was driving me nuts. I was so hurt and distraught over what had happened to you, that I thought, I thought…" she bowed her head and big teardrops fell from her eyes, splashing on the asphalt.

Voss placed his curled finger under her chin and tilted her head upwards, saying. "Are you saying you were thinking about killing yourself if I had died, just so we could be together again?"

Yada nodded yes and said, "Yeah. I know that sounds crazy, but it's true. To me, this world ain't worth living in if I don't have you by my side."

"You not crazy, ma, I feel the same way that you do. And I woulda done that shit too, if it meant that you and I would be back together again." He told her, meaning every word that he'd said to her. "Once this is all over, and I got the empire again, we gon' have us a gang of shorties and raise us a beautiful family. Right now, I just need you to hold it down while I run up this check. After that, I'ma slide back out here and put the smash down on that bitch made ass nigga Jabar. You got my word, babe. It's gon' be all about you, once this bullshit through. Just hold a nigga down, you feel me? Do what chu gotta do to keep that nigga's attention focused on something else while I'm down in Vegas getting up this money and readying the troops. Can you do that for me, lil' mama, huh?" She nodded yes. He wiped the tears that fell from her eyes and kissed her three times on the lips. He then hugged her for what seemed like forever, kissed her one last time and walked back to Dough Boy's whip.

Yada folded her arms across her breasts, watching as Voss loaded the duffle bags inside of Dough Boy's vehicle. He walked over to the front passenger door and opened it. He was about to hop into the front passenger seat, but what Yada said next stalled him.

"I love you, Voss. Make sure you come back to me."

"I love you too. And when I come back, we gon' live happily ever after."

Having said this, Voss hopped into the front passenger seat and slammed the door shut. He then gave Dough Boy the hand signal to drive off. He obliged him.

Yada waited until her lover and his best friend were out of the parking lot, before she hopped inside of her whip and drove out of there as well.

CHAPTER FIVE
Later that night

Maul and LeLe walked out of AMC theaters hand in hand after seeing CREED II.

"What's wrong, babe? You looked like something has been bothering you since we've gotten here." LeLe questioned with genuine concern.

"Nothing. I'll be all right," Maul walked beside her, hands stuffed inside of his pockets, kicking an empty *Coca Cola* can he came across on the ground. From the expression on his face, it was obvious that something was on his mind that he didn't really want to tell LeLe about.

"Something is up, babe. I can tell by the look on your face. Spit it out now, you know how we get down. We don't keep shit from one another," she said as she hooked her arm with his arm, continuing her stroll beside them. They crossed people at the carnival that were coming and going.

Maul glanced up at the sky and took a deep breath before telling her what was eating him. "You know my mom's is in the hospital, right? Well, she doing bad right now, real bad. As a matter of fact, they said if she doesn't get the heart transplant soon then she's not gonna make it. The waiting list is hella long. And by the time they get to my OG, she'll have been done went to the other side. My only saving grace is this doctor. He told me if I could get my hands on a hunnit and fifty bands then he could see to it that my mom's was bumped up on the list so she can get the surgery. The only problem is…"

"You don't have a hunnit and fifty kay?" LeLe finished his statement for him.

"Right. My pockets are tapped. And the brothas at the club pitched in, but that only gave me about fifty grand. So I'll needa hunnit more. Otherwise, that's it for my mother." Maul's eyes grew glassy and he looked like he was on the verge of crying. Seeing the sorrowful look on his face made LeLe feel sorry for him; she'd never seen him so disheveled.

"Well, I've got twenty-five grand in my savings if it'll help." LeLe told him. It was all the money she had in the world but she was willing to give up every last red cent of it if it meant it would save her boo's mom's life.

"Thank you, sweetheart, but that's still notta 'nough." Maul continued to walk alongside his lady, staring down at the ground, thinking on his situation. When he went to see his mother at the hospital she looked very weak and ill. He could tell her health was seriously declining, and she was counting on him to do something about it, even if she didn't say so. His queen was counting on him to pull off a miracle, so he had to make something happen, and fast. "Man, if I could just get my hands on some work, I know I could run up a check to pay to get mom's bumped up on that list." Suddenly, Maul brought his head up, looking like he had a bright idea. He looked to LeLe and said, "Say, do you think you could holla at cha boy, Jabar, and...ah, never mind. I couldn't ask you to do that shit for me. What am I thinking?" Maul shook his head. He couldn't believe the favor he was about to ask LeLe to do for him. He quickly shook the thought from his brain.

"Bae, don't be like that. You know if I can help you in any way I will. Just tell me." LeLe pled her case.

"I was thinking maybe you could holla at Jabar and see if he'd hit me off with a couple of them thangz. I can call a few people and put a few dollars together so I can get at least three. I'm hoping he'll front me in the other three."

LeLe thought on it for a moment. She was okay with Jabar, but she didn't know how he'd react if she asked him for a favor like the one that Maul was asking him for. She figured the worse he could say is no if she asked so she decided to holler at him for her man.

"Alright, I'll see about talking to him tonight. I'm not promising you nothing, but hopefully he'll come through so you can get cho mother that operation."

Maul smiled from ear to ear, cupping LeLe's face, he kissed her lips and then her forehead. "Thank you, baby, I really, really appreciate you doing this for me. And I'm sure momma does too."

"Don't mention it. Now, let's go get some ice cream," LeLe grabbed him by his hand and moved towards the parking lot.

The next day

When they entered the area of town that Dough Boy's people regulated in Las Vegas, Voss couldn't find a nigga out there that wasn't gripped up. It looked like Iraq out that bitch. Them niggaz was carrying bangaz out in the open like it was the Wild, Wild West or some shit. And if they weren't then you could see their guns bulging underneath their shirts. On top of that, they all looked like they were banging. And if they weren't then they were at least gang related or affiliated to some extent. Niggaz and bitchez were tatted up and wearing street attire, red baseball caps, bandanas, jerseys, Dickie suits and belt buckles to show their affiliation. Voss hadn't seen no shit like that since, like, the mid-nineties or early two-thousands.

The Bloods were serving dopefiends out in the open like it wasn't nothing. There were dopeheads running back and forth across the trashy street, going to cop heroin or having already copped heroin. Shit, there were even some of them sitting on the curb shooting up, or on their feet leaning and shit. Everything appeared to be unorganized, like them niggaz had free reign to do whatever they damn well pleased. This made Voss worry a little. You know, entering a part of the city without a governing body. A free zone if you will.

Voss was on high alert. He knew that Dough Boy said that these were his people, but fuck that. He didn't feel safe without his banga out. So he took his shit from underneath the seat and sat it in his lap, just in case niggaz wanted to get stupid.

"What chu doing, P?" Dough Boy looked back and forth between the windshield and Voss, brows crinkled.

"Man, these niggaz running around here strapped. It's only right that I hold on to my shit."

"I told you these are my people, kid. You ain't got shit to worry about."

"Dough, you been my nigga forever and a day. I trust you with my life. Your word is platinum with me. But I don't trust this situation we're about to enter. I'm sure you understand that." He glanced over at him to see the expression on his face.

Dough Boy thought on it for a second and then nodded. Once he looked over the area that they were entering again, he understood exactly where his homeboy was coming from.

Dough Boy glanced at the side view mirror and saw a nigga on a miniature bike speeding up towards them. Dough Boy slowed up to let him catch up with them. Homeboy came up beside him, and he got his first good look at him. He was youthful looking cat, about sixteen to seventeen years of age. He was of a brown hue and had a slight mustache. Tattoo on the side of his neck was Baby Rampage. The young nigga was wearing a red Cardinals fitted cap and a matching jersey which was opened to his bare chest. The strap of an M-16 was lying across his chest.

"Dough Boy, what's up wit it, Blood?" Baby Rampage said as he drove alongside the car.

"What's popping, Damu? I slid through to see that nigga Rampage about some business. Where Blood at?" Dough Boy asked him.

"Hold up." The young nigga revved up his motorbike and sped ahead of Dough Boy. He stopped up at the driveway of an apartment complex and pointed up the driveway at an apartment unit on the first floor. He then held up six fingers letting Dough Boy know that Big Rampage was inside of the unit with that number on it.

Dough Boy pulled his car inside of the apartment complex's parking lot and parked at the back of the tenement. He and Voss jumped out and made their way to the front of the building. As they neared the bottom of the staircase to the unit Rampage stayed in, they found two pit bulls with big ass heads. They were dyed red and had pink noses. Voss's forehead wrinkled up wondering which one of those crazy ass Bloods out front had dyed those goddamn dogs red.

Blood, these Vegas niggaz are burnt out, Voss thought as he shook his head. He was all good with representing the movement, but some niggaz took it to the extreme.

Woof, woof, woof, woof!
Woof, woof, woof, woof!

The dogs went wild on the red leashes once they saw Voss and Dough Boy walking up on them. The fellas made sure to keep their distance from the angry hounds.

Moving counter clock wise from them, they noted that the pit bulls were blocking the staircase. A second later, the black iron door of the staircase opened. A big buff ass nigga stepped out, smoking a blunt with an AR-15 assault rifle hoisted over his shoulder. He had a bunch of tattoos on his face and a few on his body. His eyes were covered by round lenses. He sported a nappy Mohawk which he'd dyed red and a red beard he had braided into a ponytail. He was in camouflage tank top, matching cargo pants and black boots with red shoe strings in them. He also had a Taurus .9mm handgun tucked in the front of his pants, looking like he was ready for war and shit.

"Dough Boy, what's up, Blood?" Rampage cracked a smile.

"Ain't shit. You gon' let us up or what, dawg?" Dough Boy shot back at him.

"Fa sho', loved one." Rampage turned his attention to his barking ass pit bulls. He spat some shit in Swahili to them and they sat down and shut right the fuck up.

Without the dogs to worry about, Voss and Dough Boy cautiously made their way pass the pit bulls and up the staircase. Once they'd crossed the threshold inside of the apartment unit, Rampage came in behind them, shutting and locking the door. He placed the blunt in his mouth and dapped up Voss once Dough Boy had introduced him. Rampage gave Dough Boy a gangsta hug and passed him the blunt from out of his mouth, blowing out the last of the smoke.

"Y'all niggaz have a seat, Blood. Make yo self at home, shit." Rampage motioned towards the couch which was sitting before a 70 inch 4K flat screen. *Brooklyn's Finest* was playing on the television's screen.

Sitting on the couch beside Dough Boy, Voss took in the décor of Rampage's crib. Everything in that mothafucka was red, the furniture, the walls, the curtains and the carpet. Even all the appliances inside of the kitchen were red. The rug, the stove, the towels on the stove's handle, the refrigerator as well as everything else was red also. *Talk about over doing it!*

Rampage pulled out his .9mm handgun and sat it on the coffee table. He then laid his AR-15 down across his lap, turning towards Voss and Dough Boy.

"Reli, tell my nigga the shit you and me were chopping it up about the last time a nigga was down here." Dough Boy told Rampage as he blew smoke from his nose and mouth.

"Check this out, Voss. I'm not one to pull a nigga's chain. I like to keep it one-hunnit and fiddy around this bitch. You feel me?" Rampage started off. Voss nodded so he continued on, "I got some work, but it's some bullshit. My plug got popped so I started dealing with this Mexican nigga outta town. And his shit ain't hitting on nothing, I fucked around and ran off most of my clientele messing with this dude. The fiends are looking scarce out there. From what I hear, they're fucking with them boys from across town, but that's only 'cause they're slinging seven dollar bags of dope. We're pumping ours at eight a pop. I can't afford to go lower than that. Any lower than that, then I may as well bend over and stick a dildo up my ass 'cause I'll be fucking myself, you feel me, Blood?"

Voss nodded as he massaged his chin, thinking things over. "So, you pretty much got this part of Vegas sewn up, right?"

"Yep. I got the soldiers, and the dope fiends, all that's missing is the product. If I get my hands on that, it ain't no stopping me." He nodded. "From what my relative tells me, you the nigga I needa fuck with if I plan on getting my hands on anything worthy."

"I can get my hands on some good dope. You ain't even gotta worry about that. Just limme make a phone call so I can see about getting the shit."

Voss hit up his boy Ricky he was locked up with. Ricky was slinging dope while on lock, and had mad niggaz jealous because he was snatching all of their customers with the superior dope he had. A couple of cars tried to get at him, but Voss and his band of Pirus held him down, off the strength that Voss and Ricky were cell mates. Voss's loyalty earned him favor with Ricky and he cut him in on a piece of the action. Before he was granted parole, Ricky told him if he ever needed a plug on the outside that he would take care of him and give him a good price on the shit. The situation with the Bloods out in Vegas was the perfect time for Voss to call in his marker.

"Alright, my nigga said he can meet us tomorrow afternoon. One o'clock." Voss said after checking his cellular. He'd just gotten a text back from that nigga Ricky.

"Bool," Rampage smacked his hands together and rubbed them greedily. He knew his part of Sin City was about to be popping with the good dope he was about to have on deck. "Yo man came through, relative." He looked to Dough Boy smiling.

"I told you my nigga official, Blood." Dough Boy told him with Kush smoke caged in his lungs. Smoke wafted around him as passed the smoldered blunt back to his cousin.

"Sho you, right." Rampage took the blunt and hit it.

***

Dough Boy and Ricky's carrier rented identical Suburban trucks and met up at Denny's restaurant. They ate dinner and chopped it up for about an hour before switching keys and going on about their business. Dough Boy took the Suburban back to the zone that the Bloods controlled and unloaded the product at an apartment unit on the first floor of a different tenement than the one that Rampage stayed at.

Voss put a couple of samples of the dope inside of some foil for the dope fiends to try, but they weren't fucking with it. You see, they'd never had none of the new shit that Voss was trying to sell them, and they didn't want to fuck with it for fear that it would be weak and they'd wasted their money. With that in mind, they stuck with the dope they knew, and that was, *Red Rage,* the shit that Rampage was supplying them with. When Voss was about to say fuck it and give away some of the sample for free, Rampage wasn't having it. The way he saw it they would be giving away some good dope for nothing, when they could be making a profit off of it.

Rampage was able to convince Voss to let him have a dopefiend of his choosing try the shit to prove to the others that they had some supreme work on their hands.

"Alright, I got just the old head, too." Rampage said as he rubbed his hands together in anticipation of which dopefiend he was going to hand pick for the job. His eyes scanned the streets, looking over the dopefiends running back and forth through the streets, copping and looking to cop heroin. "Yo, Big Mark, come here, Blood!" he motioned over the dopefiend the hood knew as Big Mark. Shortly, a six-foot-one fat cat lumbered over to them. He was light-skinned with short curly, gray hair, beady eyes, a pointy nose and a mouth that was missing its top row of teeth. He was wearing an apple jack hat, windbreaker over a plaid shirt, suspenders and jeans.

"What's up, Rampage?" Big Mark greeted him, scratching his armpit.

"You tryna get high, Big Dawg?" Rampage asked seriously, holding up foil of dope.

"Hell yeah!" Big Mark's eyes got as big as saucers at the mention of dope.

"I'ma let chu have this, but only on one condition." Rampage told him.

"Anything, man, I needa get right. And real fast too, I think I'm fitsna be sick."

"When you find out how fiyah this shit is, you tell all yo friends. Deal?"

"You got it, black man."

"Here you go," Rampage held out the foil of dope and Big Mark snatched it.

Voss, Dough Boy and Rampage watched as Big Mark ran over into the corner of the apartment complex where a few dopeheads were either getting high or trying to piece up a couple of dollars so they could buy some dope.

"What chu got there, Big Mark?" a scrawny dopefiend asked.

"Just some new shit Rampage blessed me with. I heard it's the business," Big Mark said pulling up a blue milk crate and sitting down on it. Most of the dopefiends eyeballed him as he opened up a worn, brown leather case he'd been carrying around like a folder and unzipped it. Inside of the case were all of the items he'd needed to administer a shot of heroin. Once he was done preparing the needle full of dope, he looked at the shaft of the syringe, thumping it with his fingers. Big Mark skeeted some of the drug out from the sharp tip of the needle, and sat it down on his leg. At this time the dopeheads who didn't have any drugs were looking at the needle of dope with lustful eyes, rubbing their hands together greedily.

Big Mark went on to unbuckle his belt and pull it free from the loops of his jeans. He then rolled up the sleeve of his shirt, chewing on his tongue as he performed the task at hand. He looped the belt around his arm and buckled it, pulling it tightly. He then tapped the inside of his arm causing a thick ass vein to rise, bulging upward. Big Mark's eyes focused on the vein in his arm as he picked up the syringe. He brought the needle of his syringe downward, piercing his vein. The moment the syringe entered his flesh, a cloud of crimson blood rushed inside of the needle, tainting its contents to a 14k gold color. As the hefty dopefiend pushed the heroin inside of his arm, he used his other hand to unbuckle his belt and relieve the tightness from around his chubby arm.

Once the dope reached Big Mark's bloodstream, his eyes rolled to their whites and he threw his head back. His hand fell beside him and he dropped the syringe he'd used to shoot the dope with. A smile spread across his big chapped lips, revealing his missing top row of teeth once again. He looked like he was experiencing euphoria. But, suddenly his eyes bulged and his body went limp. He fell back off of the milk crate and busted his ass. Big Mark's eyelids fluttered with whiteness. His lips turned bluish black and his heart thudded harder than usual. The hefty dopefiend breathed erratically. He started making gurgling noises from his throat and foam ran out of the side of his mouth, dripping on the ground. As his body went through convulsions, the dopeheads exchanged glances and looked down at him with wide eyes. Abruptly, Big Mark's convulsing stopped, and his head rolled to the side, staying still.

One of the dopefiends that was in middle of shooting up, pulled the needle from out of his arm. With his belt still dangling from his arm, he walked over to Big Mark and placed two of his fingers at the pulse on the side of his neck. His big ass was dead!

"This nigga dead!" the dopefiend announced.

"Fuck kinda dope he had?" another dopefiend asked.

"I don't know, but that shit must be the truth!" a third dopefiend said. He then grabbed the foil that Big Mark had gotten the heroin in and started licking up the residue that was left in it.

"Man, fuck that! I want some of that shit." The dopefiend that had checked Big Mark's pulse said, removing the belt from around his arm.

"Me, too, fuck he get it from?" A forth dopefiend inquired.

"Over there," the dopefiend that had just taken the belt from around his arm pointed to the apartment unit that Voss, Dough Boy and Rampage were standing at. "I think that nigga Rampage gave it to 'em."

The dopefiends gathered up with their buying dollars and moved to purchase what they believed was the best dope in the hood. Shit was crazy. You would think a nigga dropping dead off of heroin would make mothafuckaz not want to fuck with it. But that wasn't the case with these hypes. Nah, the way they looked at it, if a fiend dropped dead off the *Boy,* then it had to have been some good shit.

Dough Boy opened up one of the foils that contained the dope, looking down at it. "What're we gon' stamp this shit?" he asked Voss.

"Hmmm," Voss said in deep thought, thinking about what he should call his new product, massaging his chin. He was pacing the ground back and forth. While he was doing this, Rampage was talking to the dopefiends about the dope that Big Mark had overdosed on.

A nigga tryna knock this bitch ass nigga Jabar off the throne, and regain the top dawg status that I feel is rightfully mine. That within itself is a power move. This whole thang we doing is about power, so it's only right that I name it...

Voss stopped pacing and turned around to Dough Boy, saying, "Power!"

"What chu say, P?" Dough Boy inquired, not quite hearing what his best friend had said.

"We gon' call this shit Power, Blood." He then pointed at the foil of dope that Dough Boy was holding. "Niggaz dropping dead off this dope so fiends gon' love it. I'm telling you, P, this new shit 'bouta shake up Vegas. And me and yo peoples is about to make a hell of a lotta money."

A smiling Dough Boy switched hands with the foil of dope and gave Voss a complex handshake, saying, "Now, that's the kinda shit a nigga wanna hear."

CHAPTER SIX

Voss rented out an apartment unit from a building across the street and turned that bitch into a heroin lab. That's right, he had fifteen butt naked bitchez in their stretching the heroin he'd copped from Ricky with a cutting agent. Those hoes up in there were wearing surgical masks, latex gloves and white aprons. Other than those articles of clothing, those chicks were naked up in there. Their ass and their titties were out. Voss didn't trust a mothafucking soul not to steal. Hell, he even took extra precautions by having five of Rampage's Blood homies stand guard over them with AK-47s with one-hundred round drums.

Anyway, Voss had them butt naked broads up there using Levamisole to cut the dope with. The Levamisole was used to stretch the product so they could make more profit off of it. Adding the Levamisole didn't fuck up the work though. It actually helped to stop the dope-fiends from dropping dead from off the heroin. The shit was too potent before then.

Voss was making a killing off of serving *Power*. He and his crew had more money than they knew what to do with. The streets and Rampage's faction of Bloods loved that nigga like cooked food. They watched over him and protected him like he was the mothafucking president. He was like the goose that laid the golden egg and they couldn't allow anything to happen to him because he had the plug on the dope that gave their hood life again.

With Voss's new serge of money, niggaz on the other side started losing money. You see, the fiends that were fucking with them started fucking with the Bloods because they had the superior product. The Crips didn't like this. Nah, in fact, they hated that shit. So it was only a matter of time that they had to see about making some changes on their part so they could eat just as good as the Bloods were eating.

Voss, Dough Boy and Rampage stood at the beginning of the driveway of the apartment complex, watching everything going on before them. The scene was just like it was when Voss and Dough Boy first rolled up. Niggaz and bitchez were walking around with their guns, drinking, smoking, partying and serving dopefiends out in the open like it wasn't a thang. It really fucked Voss up when he looked down the block and saw a police car coast past, looking dead at the Bloods doing whatever the fuck they wanted to. He started to alert Rampage to what the fuck he saw, but the muscle bound Blood had already peeped they had police presence.

"Relax, my nigga, we good in the hood." Rampage told him in his ear in a hushed tone.

"I meant to ask you, how are y'all able to be out here with all these guns, getting high and serving fiends in broad daylight like it's legal and shit." Voss looked at him with curiosity plastered across his face.

"Shiiiit, Blood, I gotta quarter of the police force out here on my payroll." Rampage put him in the know. "Long as we keep the bodies we drop to a minimum, we can pretty much do whatever the fuck we want." Voss nodded his understanding and went back to watching the scenery.

Right then, Baby Rampage sped to a stop on a miniature motorbike before Voss, Dough Boy and Rampage. "Yo, big homie," the little nigga addressed Rampage. "Some crabs came through to chop it up with you. We got 'em holed up down the block; it's up to you if you wanna entertain whatever it is they got to say."

Rampage, Voss and Dough Boy looked up the block at two Crips. One was in a gray Dickie suit and blue

Chuck Taylors while the other was in a white T-shirt and jean shorts. The one in the Dickie suit was Geezy and the other in the white T-shirt was Rocco.

Rampage locked eyes with Geezy. Geezy threw his head back like *What's up?* They remembered one another from their last meeting. They'd come together to broker a peace treaty between their two warring parties. Remembering this, Rampage decided to listen to what homeboy had to say.

"Alright, let 'em through, but pat they asses down first." Rampage told his little homeboy.

"Alright," Baby Rampage revved up his bike and busted a U-turn, driving back up on his homeboys and Geezy and Rocco. Rampage watched as Baby Rampage spat something at his homies who proceeded to give the Crips a thorough pat down. Afterwards, the Crips were granted their conversation with Rampage. When they rolled up everybody slapped hands with them, except for Dough Boy. He mad dogged them mothafuckaz, sizing them up.

"My nigga, what's yo problem?" Rocco asked Dough Boy, frowned up.

"You my problem, mothafucka!" Dough Boy spat fire. He was about to step to Rocco, but Rampage placed his arm across his chest, halting him.

"Fallback, reli, let's hear 'em out." Rampage said to his cousin.

Dough Boy took a step back, but kept mad dogging Rocco. He didn't like Crips for shit. Far as he was concerned they were the enemies. He didn't have any love for them. Fuck them!

"Salute to you and yours, my nigga. Y'all doing y'all thang down here," Geezy addressed Rampage, looking around at all of the dopefiends shuffling around buying Power.

"My nigga, enough with the small talk, exactly what is it that chu want?" Rampage folded his big muscular arms across his chest and frowned up. From the expression on his face you could tell that he wasn't feeling the Crips' presence, and would be glad once he got the fuck on from around him. The only reason why he hadn't had them popped was because he and their shot caller, God Body, had declared a cease fire and peace treaty so the two sides could get money in peace.

Geezy took a breath before going on with what he had to say. "Well, first off, congratulations on yo success. I ain't never hadda problem with saluting a nigga for doing his thang, homie or enemy. Me and my nigga, Rocco, came down here in hopes that we could buy yo plug from off you so we can get some of this money out here, too."

Rampage exchanged glances with Voss and Dough Boy, then he looked back to Geezy. Abruptly, he busted up laughing, doubling over and slapping his leg. The buff ass nigga laughed so hard that you would have thought he'd just heard the most hilarious joke ever. He then brought his head back up, looking as serious as a heart attack, he said, "My nigga, y'all seeing y'all not eating like y'all used to since we gotta superior product now, now y'all wanna buy into our shit so we can split all this money out here equally? Nah, homeboy," Rampage shook his head no. "I can't believe y'all, man. Y'all must think we on some sucka shit down here. We're not sharing our plug with nobody! Fuck that! Y'all niggaz breeze, man." Rampage threw his head in the direction that the Crips came from, and then he spat on the ground.

"Well, look, how about..." Geezy was cut short when Dough Boy stepped into his face with his banga down at his side Like *Blood, what's bracking?*

"Blood, you heard my relative, y'all bitches kick rocks 'fore the fireworks come out early 'round this bitch!" Dough Boy mad dogged Geezy and gritted his teeth, looking like the mean son of a bitch that he really was.

Geezy smiled and lifted his hands in the air, surrendering. "We don't want no trouble, bruh. Just thought we'd dip through for a peaceful conversation is all."

"Conversation over, Blood, take yo girlfriend and get the fuck from 'round here!" Dough Boy kicked him in the ass and he nearly fell. Geezy's face balled up with anger and he wanted to fire on Dough Boy but he was sure if he did that he'd kill him. With that in mind, he nudged Rocco and told him to come on as they headed back towards their vehicle. Once they were out of sight, Dough Boy tucked his gun on his waistline.

"Them two niggaz are brazy, Blood. I know they know betta than to come and ask me that shit. Who in their right mind would give up there plug to their competition?" Rampage shook his head, like he couldn't believe the audacity of the Crips.

"Niggaz must really be fucked up down that way, bro. Them blue rags threw their pride outta the window coming down here, and that ain't easy for no man to do." Voss finally spoke up again.

Vrooom!

Baby Rampage sped up the street and came to a stop on the sidewalk in front of Rampage.

"What them niggaz wanted, Blood?" Baby Rampage asked his big homie.

"Niggaz tryna buy the plug from us." Rampage replied, looking down the block to see Geezy and Rocco pulling off in a navy blue Durango truck. He looked back to Baby Rampage to see what he had to say.

"Shiiiiit, them fools must be shooting up this shit we slinging out here to believe you was gon' come off that." Baby Rampage pulled his Newport from behind his ear and stuck it inside of his mouth. He then rifled through his pockets for a lighter, brows furrowing when he didn't come up with one. "Yo, one of y'all niggaz gotta light, Blood?"

"Yeah, I got chu." Voss pulled his Bic lighter from out of his pocket and struck a flame. A blue flame with a yellow tip licked at the air until it was brought to the tip of the young nigga'z cigarette. Once the tip of the Newport was ember and wafting smoke, Voss put his lighter away. As soon as Baby Rampage thanked him, his head exploded and specks of blood clinged to Voss's face and clothing. Voss, Dough Boy and Rampage looked up. They saw Rocco hanging halfway out of the window with a chrome .357 Magnum revolver, wafting with smoke. He ducked back inside of the Durango truck, and Geezy sped off. A bunch of the Bloods, including Dough Boy and Rampage ran out into the streets, guns drawn. They pointed their guns at the fleeing Durango truck and opened fire, shattering the back window of the SUV and putting holes in its rear. Rampage, Dough Boy and the rest of the Bloods lowered their guns seeing that the Durango had gotten too far for them to hit.

While all of this was going on, Voss was standing over Baby Rampage's dead body, looking at the horror etched across his youthful face. His eyes were big and his mouth was hanging open. A chunk of flesh and skull was missing from out of the back of his head. Blood pooled around his dome and dripped off of the curb, while his motorbike's engine continued to run.

***

"Rampage, I know yo people out there screaming murder, but it's like you said, the police agreed to let chu operate out here as long as you kept the bodies to a minimum." Voss told him. "If we ride back on these fools then its fa sho' gon' kick off an all-out-war."

"I hear you talking, my nigga. But do you have another way we can get at these fools?" Rampage asked him.

"I gotta way we can get even for Baby Rampage and get these niggaz to shop with us."

"Well, let's hear it." Rampage told him.

"Yeah, P, don't keep an asshole in suspense." Dough Boy chimed in.

Voss went on to tell Rampage and Dough Boy about his plan. He told them that they were going to agree to let the Crips buy the plug from off of them. They were also going to give a peace offering to their shot-caller, God Body, as a show of good gesture. The peace offering would be two women. And the women they send would assassinate God Body since he was the only nigga with the plug on the dope his people was selling. The Crips would have to come to them to buy their dope which they would jack the price up on. This would be the only way that the Crips would get their hands on Power, because they sure as hell wasn't about to sell those mothafuckaz their plug. Voss was sure that the Crips would go for it because with Power they didn't stand a chance to make any real money.

"You smart as a mothafucka, Blood." Dough Boy told Voss as he poured up a glass of Hennessy.

"That's a good idea. But I met God Body once at a strip club. Blood, didn't fuck with any of those bitchez in there that had tattoos or weaves. He hated those kinda females." Rampage told him. "And unfortunately, those are the only kinda bitchez I know down here. We'd have to get us a couple of broads that's fine as wine, rocking their own hair and don't have any tattoos."

"Hmmm," Voss massaged his chin as he thought on it. He then looked to Rampage and said, "I can see about getting my wife and her girl to do it."

"How they look?" Rampage inquired.

"Hold up." Voss pulled out his wallet and showed Rampage a picture of him and Yada, and then one of Yada and LeLe.

"Yeah, wifey and her girl are bad. Real bad." Rampage said, staring down at the picture. His eyes lingered on the picture a little longer before he handed it back to Voss to put back inside of his wallet.

"So, we all agree to let wifey and her girl bust this move?" Voss looked around at Rampage and Dough Boy as he shoved his wallet into his back pocket. Dough Boy and Rampage nodded. "Good, I'ma see what's up with 'em once they come down here tomorrow night. In the meantime, Rampage, holla at God Body and put that offer on the table."

"Alright," Rampage grabbed his cell phone from off the coffee table and headed inside of his bedroom to use it.

Voss sat down on the couch beside Dough Boy who'd started smoking a blunt about a minute to go. Dough Boy passed the blunt to him and he took a couple of puffs, blowing out a big ass cloud of smoke.

"Yo, so, you think this plan gon' work?" Dough Boy inquired.

"I hope so, my nigga. I hope so." He took a couple of more puffs and then passed the blunt back to his right-hand man.

***

Jabar was staring at a portrait of him, Lyndell, Voss, Yada and LeLe when he heard a knock at the door of his study. He cleared his throat, sat the portrait back down on his desk top and looked to Bang, nodding to him. This was his signal to open the door. Bang hopped to his feet and made his way towards the door of the study, which he opened. Maul waltzed in and stopped at the desk. Once Bang closed the door behind him, he called him back over to him. Maul stepped before Bang and outstretched his arms and legs like he told him. He then patted him down thoroughly for any wires which he didn't find on him. Once Bang had finished his pat down of Maul, he gave Jabar a nod which let him know that homeboy was as clean as a whistle. He then left out of the study, pulling the door shut behind him.

Maul cleared his throat and said, "Thanks for seeing me."

"Fa sho'," Jabar replied with his attention focused down in the antique cigar box. He pulled out one and placed it inside of his mouth. "You wanna cigar? They're Cuban."

"No thank you."

"Suit yourself." He shut the cigar box and clipped the tip off of his cigar. He then whipped out his Zippo lighter and struck a bluish flame with a yellow tip, roasting the end of the cigar until it was an ember. He sucked on the end of the cigar and blew out a big ass cloud of smoke. Afterwards, he walked around to the front of his desk and leant up against it, continuously indulging in the cancerous tobacco smoke. "Let's get this straight. I don't know you and you damn sho' don't know me. The only reason I'm entertaining this conversation is on the strength of LeLe. She practically begged me to take this meeting. And being that she and I are alright, I felt the need to oblige her."

Maul nodded and said, "I understand."

"Good. Now she said you're looking to cop three while I front you the other three. Did I understand her correctly?"

"Yeah, that's right." He nodded.

"Okay. Cool. I can do that." Jabar took the time to remove the cigar out of his mouth and blow out another cloud of smoke. "You got the money now?"

"I got it, but it's not with me." Maul admitted. "I figured once it came time to make the exchange that I'd bring it along."

Jabar nodded as he gnawed on the end of the cigar. "That's fine."

"Listen, I hate to be the type of nigga you give an inch but he tries to take a foot. But I've gotta ask you for just one more favor."

Jabar rolled his eyes and blew his hot breath. Maul had him irritated as fuck. Niggaz always wanted a handout. They never wanted to work for shit. They just wanted it given to them on a silver platter. Holding the cigar between his fingers, he scratched his temple with his thumb. "Boyyyy, you can't do shit for niggaz these days without them wanting more than they're willing to give. I'll tell ya, the fucking world we live in today, dawg." He said to himself, under his breath before addressing Maul. "Sho', man! What is it that chu want me to do?"

"I want chu to die, cocksucka!" Maul's face balled up and he clenched his jaws, causing the vein at his temple to twitch angrily. He reached inside of his locs which were pinned up in a bun and pulled out two sharp ass knives, that resembled steak knives. As soon as he did, his locs fell loose over his shoulders and back. Jabar's eyes bulged and his mouth hung open, seeing the hulk of a man lunge forward with the knives. He moved out of the way just as he was bringing one of the knives down in a stabbing motion. Thock! The knife wedge inside of the desk top, and Maul yanked it free. He charged at Jabar, swinging the knives rapidly, trying to stab and poke him.

Snikt, snikt, snikt, snikt!

Jabar moved with the grace of a ballerina, dodging the knives but getting the front of his shirt sliced in ribbons while in the process. He fucked around and made a wrong move, and Maul took advantage of it. He swung his knife downward. The lethal blade ripped through the flesh of his shoulder and stabbed into his bone. Jabar made an ugly ass face as he screamed bloody murder.

"Raahhhhhh!" Jabar's mouth opened so wide from screaming that you could see every tooth and cavity inside of his grill.

"You got my homeboy, Johnny, shot! And you gave the order to kill my cousin, mothafucka!" Maul gritted with extreme hatred. He took a swipe at Jabar with his other knife twice, but he managed to avoid the blade. Maul then punched him with his left, then his right and kicked him square in the chest. The impact sent Jabar's ugly ass flying backwards, slamming into the glass display case that housed several rifles. The glass of the case shattered and broken glass rained down on the carpet. A dizzy Jabar dropped down on his ass, sitting on the broken glass. Seeing that the poor bastard was at his mercy, Jabar casually strolled toward him, with his last knife. He was going to slit his throat from ear to ear. "It's time to kiss yo black ass good buy, homie." He spat on the carpeted floor as he advanced in Jabar's direction. Reaching him, he pulled him up to the tips of his sneakers by the collar of his shirt. Jabar's eyes were rolled to their whites and he was moaning in pain. Maul held the knife back in a swiping motion. Right when he was about to slash his enemy's throat, the left side of his head exploded and speckles of blood dotted Jabar's face.

Maul collapsed to the floor lifelessly, dropping Jabar in the process. When they dropped out of sight, Bang was shown behind them, holding his gun as it wafted with smoke. Scowling, he lowered his banga, and strolled over to Maul. Stopping before him, looked down at his wide eyes and opened mouth. He looked horrified when he died.

"I knew something was up with this bitch ass nigga!" Bang shook his head. He then clapped Maul two more times. *Blowl! Blowl!*

Bang looked up to see Jabar wincing as he pulled Maul's knife out of his shoulder, tossing it aside. Banga tucked his warm banga on his waistline and helped him up. Heated that homeboy really tried to take him out, Jabar walked up on Maul and kicked him in his side.

"Fuck was this all about, dawg?" Bang asked Jabar.

"Nigga said I gave the order to have his cousin killed. So it must have something to do with that message I told you to send to them BDOG's who were slanging over there off of San Pedro."

Bang looked at Maul closely with a furrowed forehead, turning his head from left to right. He narrowed his eyelids into slits trying to picture him as another raise. "Them mothafuckaz we put the love on was Mexicans, every last one of them. That, I'm sure of, this nigga must be mixed."

Jabar looked at Maul carefully. "Yeah, he looked like he could be half Spanish or some shit. See if this nigga gotta brand." He said, referring to the BDOG tattoo that all members had.

Bang kneeled down to Maul's corpse and checked his neck and both of his arms. He found several tattoos that represented his Venom's motorcycle club affiliation, but he hadn't found any ink that showed he was down with BDOG. It wasn't until he lifted up his right jean's leg that he found his BDOG tattoo, which was in its beginning stages of fading.

"And there you have it ladies and gentlemen," Bang said of Maul's tattoo as he stared down at it. He then looked up at Jabar. "You said LeLe plugged you in with this nigga, right? You think lil' mama had something to do with this shit?"

"I can't call it, my nigga. But I do intend to find out." Jabar exclaimed and then spit on Maul's face. "Call Tankhead and Rondo, so they can help you get this piece of shit outta here."

"Fa sho'." Bang pulled out his cell phone and made the call.

***

"I need you and LeLe to bust this move for a nigga, babe." Voss told Yada. She and LeLe had came out of the apartment that Voss had a dopefiend rent out while he was doing business in Las Vegas, Nevada. At the moment LeLe was sitting in the living room with Dough Boy and Rampage getting high. Yada had just came into Voss's bedroom from taking a few drags from off a blunt.

"What's the issue, lover?" Yada's face balled up with concern for her man.

Voss gave her the run down on what he and the Bloods out in Vegas was trying to do. "Now, this nigga Rampage had some broads to do it, but they aren't nearly as bad as you and LeLe. On top of that, I know my boo gon' get in there and make sure the job is done. She gon' handle her business."

"Well, look, you my man, so you know I'm down for it all when it comes to you. But I can't speak for LeLe, she gon' have to speak for herself."

"Sho' you right. Go get her for me, babe."

"Alright," Yada left the bedroom and returned with LeLe. She had a curious expression on her face.

"What's up, bro?" LeLe threw her head back.

Voss told her the plan that he and the Bloods had in mind. To sweeten the pot, he threw in fifty thousand dollars for her troubles.

"Bro, you know I fucks witchu, so if I'm gon' do this shit its gon' be on the strength. Fuck the money. You married to my sister so you family." She told him how it was with her.

A smile spread across Voss's face knowing he had two down ass chicks on his team. "So, you with the shits?"

"I'm with the shits." She nodded.

With that having been said, Voss hung his arms around Yada and LeLe's necks, kissing them on their respective cheeks. He then walked over to his dresser drawer, pulled it open and took out a photograph, handing it to LeLe. She and Yada stood shoulder to shoulder, looking over the photograph.

"Is this the nigga you want us to hit?" Yada asked her husband.

"Oooooou, he's cute." LeLe commented on his looks.

"Yeah, that's him. Name's God Body." He informed them. "He's the shot caller of them niggaz on the other side that's pushing heroin, too. He supplies 'em. So we gotta take 'em out."

"But even if you take 'em out, won't those other niggaz still be gunning after y'all?" LeLe asked.

"Maybe in the beginning, but that retaliation shit will dwindle, eventually. You see, niggaz can't war if they ain't got no paper coming in. They'll be too busy worried about how they gon' keepa roof over their heads and food on their fucking tables. You feel what I'm saying?"

"Yeah, I think so," LeLe nodded. "Kill the head and the body will follow."

Voss smirked and tapped his finger against his temple, letting her know that she was on point with her theory.

"Alright, babe," Yada handed him the photograph back of God Body. "When we hitting this Mr. God Body?"

"Tonight." He walked over to the closet and brought out two sexy dresses that he wanted them to wear to God Body's downfall. He handed them the dresses by the hanger. LeLe got the black one while Yada got the burgundy one. The ladies' eyes lit up and they smiled, loving the clothing they'd be wearing that night. While they were busy holding the dresses up against themselves, and looking themselves over in the mirror, Voss recovered the shoes from out of the closet. He gave it to them, along with a bag of sexy under garments.

"Heyyy, babe, you got chu some taste." Yada complimented with a smile, looking over the red bottom heels she'd taken out of one of the boxes of shoes Voss had given them.

"Of course, I got taste. I bagged you, didn't I?" Voss capped with a smile, folding his arms across his chest.

"He got chu with that one, girl." LeLe smiled, holding one of the shoes in her hand.

"That chu did. I can't front." Yada walked over to her husband and kissed him.

Voss looked at his watch and then back up at his wife. "Look, I'ma give y'all time to shower and get dressed. Y'all females so I know y'all gon' be like three hours up in this bitch. I'ma hit up dude's people and let 'em know we gon' slide out at, like, ten o'clock. Y'all should be ready by then, right?" he looked from LeLe to Yada, waiting for their answers.

"Yeah, we'll be ready then, babe." Yada assured him.

"Alright then. Thank you, mamas," Voss kissed Yada. He then touched fists with LeLe. "Good looking out, sis."

"Don't mention it, bro bro."

Voss left the bedroom and returned with two wine glasses and a black bottle of expensive red wine for the girls. He wanted them to be relaxed before their mission. He knew that murder was a task that wasn't easy to stomach, and he was mindful of that. He couldn't afford for them to botch the hit on God Body. He knew that if the girls dropped the ball on this one that he and the bloods would have themselves a war on his hands. And that wasn't something he was ready to deal with. He was making too much money to let something like the existence of one measly man to come along and disrupt his cash flow. *Fuck that!*

CHAPTER SEVEN

Voss stole glances at Yada and LeLe through the rear-view mirror as he drove the Benz van. A slight smirk spread across his lips seeing that the wine had the girls at ease. He could tell by the looks on their faces that they were ready to perform the task he'd assigned to them, and that made him feel confident in their skill in pulling the shit off.

Before the girls knew it, Voss was pulling through the gates of God Body's mansion. Voss drove down the path and around the circular cobble stoned driveway where there were other cars parked. Two G-wagons and a white Mercedes Benz limousine with limousine tinted windows. Voss murdered the engine of the van and looked out of the driver's window. At the end of his line of vision, he saw two African American men approaching. The first one was a baldheaded nigga in a light gray suit and the other rocked a tapered afro, and was in a navy blue suit. They were two serious looking cats, and from the way they were moving, Voss knew that they were strapped up. The baldheaded one was carrying a long rod that curved at its end and had what looked like a small mirror attached to the end of it. Voss had seen one of these kinds of tools before. Before he was bussed out of the county jail, one of the corrections officers would come out with one to check underneath the prison bus.

Bitch ass niggaz are smart. They figure my ol' gangsta ass would bust a move, and they were right, don't trust nobody. Especially a nigga raised off the Eastside of them Bottoms.

"Alright, ladies, here these mothafuckaz come," Voss told them, watching their appearance through the rearview mirror. "Remember y'all's assignment: whack that nigga and get the fuck out. I'ma be waiting down here for y'all. Don't worry about nothing, y'all got this. I gotta lot riding on this, but I'm putting my faith in y'all. The baddest bitchez there has ever been and ever will be." He said, gassing them up and stroking their ego like a smooth talking pimp.

"We got chu faded, babe. Don't worry about nothing. Me and my bitch won't let chu down." Yada said, looking in the compact mirror she'd drawn from her purse and fixing her hair. LeLe was sitting beside her, looking in her compact mirror and applying a fresh coat of lipstick to her lips.

Yada nudged LeLe so she could assure Voss that they could handle the assignment. "You don't have to worry about us, bro," LeLe assured him. "Me and wifey got this."

"I'm counting on that." Voss glanced out of his window, finding the guard with the afro standing at his door. The other one was moving alongside the van with the rod, making sure there weren't any weapons hidden underneath the vehicle. Once baldhead had finished, he looked to his counterpart and gave him a nod, which let him know that the van was clear of weapons. With that signal having been given, afro told Voss to let the girls out of the van. The girls opened the door and hopped out. They were made to face the van with their hands placed against it with their legs spread apart, like they were a couple of suspects. Baldhead stood aside with the rod while afro thoroughly searched the girls and their handbags, finding nothing. He then gave them their respective handbags back, and climbed inside of the van. He checked everything inside of the transporting vehicle, leaving no crack or crevasse unchecked.

"Goddamn, my nigga, fuck y'all guarding, the president?" Voss asked with a chuckle. When afro glanced up at the rearview mirror wearing a solemn face, the jovial expression disappeared from Voss's face. He focused his attention out of the windshield, whistling and drumming his fingers on the van's windowpane.

Once afro was done, he shut the door of the van. He then had Voss step out. He searched him, just like he'd done with the girls. Afterwards, he searched the front of the van. When he didn't come up with anything, he gave baldhead a nod, letting him know the van was clean.

Voss jumped back inside of the van and slammed the door shut behind him. He then looked out of the window, telling the girls, "I'll see y'all in about three hours. I'll be out here waiting on you." He went ahead and fired up the half smoked blunt he had on deck, blowing out a cloud of smoke. The girls looked over their shoulders as they followed behind the guards and nodded to Voss.

Once the girls and the guards disappeared through the doors of the mansion, Voss activated his stash spot and pulled out a MAC-10. He sat it on the front passenger seat along with an extra magazine. Afterwards, he shut his stash spot.

All that mothafucking searching and them rent-a-cops didn't find jack shit. Dumb and fucking Dumber, Voss chuckled to himself and took another pull from the blunt, blowing smoke into the air.

***

Yada and LeLe left Voss behind in the van, following the guards up the long flight of steps to the mansion. The first guard crossed the threshold and held open the blue door with the silver knocker for everyone else to enter. As soon as Yada and LeLe stepped foot onto the Italian imported tiled floor they were greeted by Kirk Franklin's *The Reason Why I Sing* which was playing throughout the massive dwelling.

For some that don't understand our purpose
And may not understand our praise
We as the family in Jesus name
Would like to tell you the reason why we sing, family

The guards led the girls up a spiral staircase. They stopped at twin, white double doors and one of them cleared his throat and knocked on it, saying, "Your entertainment has arrived, sir." He adjusted his tie and smoothed it out, re-buttoning his suit.

"Come in," God Body replied from the other side of the door.

Baldhead turned the golden handle of the door and pushed his way inside, crossing the threshold inside of the master bedroom. He stepped aside and allowed Yada and LeLe to enter his boss' domain. The girls made their way across the threshold, taking in the scenery surrounding them. The master bedroom was made up like an Egyptian palace and was just as spacious.

Yada and LeLe looked away from the décor of the master bedroom and focused on the six-foot-four man approaching them from the balcony. He strode forward, taking pulls from a fat ass blunt, smoke wafting around him. He opened his mouth and blew out smoke rings, allowing them to rise to the ceiling and evaporate.

God Body was very menacing and intimidating in appearance. He rocked a fade that swirled in 360 waves and a goatee that framed his mouth perfectly, thanks to him getting a haircut every three days. He had an ugly scar he'd gotten in a knife fight as a teenager that led from his forehead, over his eyelids down over his cheek. He'd gotten his name due to his Olympian physique, and the fact that he could make it snow (drop blow on dope boyz) in the middle of the summer, and his love of The Almighty. As of right now, he was wearing one of those small ass skullcaps (a zucchetto) on his head like the pope which was royal blue and silk white and royal blue cassock. His feet nestled in the shaggy mink carpet as he mashed out the blunt inside of a glass ashtray, stopping before the girls. He blew the last of the smoke from his nostrils and cracked a smile, showcasing his off pearly white teeth.

"Lock and close the door, cuz," God Body said to the guards as he sat the ashtray down on the nightstand and began disrobing.

"Yes, sir," the guard wearing the afro said, leaving the bedroom and shutting the door behind them.

Yada and LeLe kept their eyes on God Body who was peeling off the holy garments. Once his cassock dropped into a pile at his feet, the girls got a good look at the ink on his form. He had a Jesus piece necklace around his neck, a prayer hands on his left peck which had God's Got Me below it, his twin daughters faces on his right peck, Crip God across his abs, and a host of other gang tattoos that let them know he was affiliated with the Crips. When God Body finished getting undressed, he was left in his zucchetto, gun holsters that contained Desert Eagles which were strapped across his back and dangling underneath his armpits, and silk royal blue boxers which showcased his bulge.

God Body clapped his hands and Vanity's *Nasty Girl* erupted from the speakers in the high corners of the master bedroom.

Tonight I'm livin' in a fantasy
My own little nasty world
Tonight, don't you wanna come with me

Do you think I'm a nasty girl

"Do a strip tease for me!" God Body told the girls over the loud ass music. He then sat down on the bed, watching Yada and LeLe move their bodies like belly dancers, in sync with the beat of the sensual music playing. He smiled happily and rubbed his tattooed hands together, finding himself slowly getting aroused. Yada and LeLe stood before him slowly removing their clothes and dancing exotically for the man they were assigned to assassinate. Seeing that they were pleasing God Body, jovial expressions spread across their faces, before long their titties were out, but they still had on their G-strings.

"Okay, now kiss!" God Body said as loud as he could over the loud music, motioning with both of his hands. With the directions having been given, Yada and LeLe engaged one another, cupping each other's faces. Their lips pressed against one another's and they began kissing long, deep and lustfully. 'Mmmmmm's' escaped their lips as they turned their heads away from each other, kissing passionately. They were really into their making out which made God Body's dick as hard as a red bricked building. "Yeahhhh, now that's the type of shit that The God likes." He chewed his tongue and begun massaging the hardened meat in his boxers.

God Body suddenly rose from off the bed, engaging the women. He pulled them apart and had a three way kiss with them. Everyone's eyelids were shut as they performed the three way kiss. There was a lot of slopping, sucking and touching going on between them. While God Body's hands were busy groping a handful of each girl's breasts, LeLe's hand was stroking his dick gently, causing it to get harder and harder. As this was taking place, Yada was rubbing her hand up and down his chiseled chest, enjoying the muscles in it.

God Body took the girls by their hand and led them to the bed. He sat down on the bed, kissing Yada and directing LeLe towards his dick. While he was busy making out with Yada, LeLe got down on her knees and pulled his dick out of his boxers. She stroked his dick up and down causing it to grow longer and harder in her fist. The head of him throbbed and oozed with a clear fluid. LeLe admired his thick penis and the veins going up and down it, making it look masculine. Holding his dick with one hand, LeLe dipped her head below his shaft and moved something around in her mouth with the assistance of her jaws. A moment later, a Gemstar razor emerged between her teeth, gleaming below the light in the ceiling.

LeLe's eyes shifted to the biggest vein on God Body's dick. She aimed for it, and swiped the razor across it.

God Body pulled away from Yada and screamed bloody murder, mouth trembling, "Aaaaahhhhhh!" Blood squirted upwards, and the godly Crip socked the shit out of LeLe and kicked her in the stomach, flipping her over on her back. She bawled in pain holding her stomach, dripping blood from off her chin. God Body touched his bleeding dick and winced, when he looked to his hand, it was bloody. Seeing all the blood seemed to have infuriated him. His eyebrows arched and his nose squished up. Using his bloody hand, he snatched one of his Desert Eagles from its holster and aimed it at LeLe's skull. She saw him about to pull the trigger but she was in too much agony to do anything to stop him. "Fucking bitch, I'll kill you!"

Blam!

The shot went wild as Yada sliced him across his forearm with a Gemstar razor identical to the one that LeLe cut his ass with. He dropped his banga and hollered aloud. Whipping around, he backhanded Yada and she flipped off of the edge of the bed. "You black bitchez! I know y'all didn't waltz yo pretty asses in here thinking you were about to pick off the Locsta, did you? Huh? I'm God Body, bitch! Remember the name!"

At this time, the double doors of the master bedroom shook violent with the guards pounding on it trying to get in. But God Body ignored them. He was going to kill those bitchez and leave them for his security team to clean up.

God Body pulled out his other Desert Eagle and went to put a bullet in LeLe's brain. Before he could deliver the kill-shot, Yada picked up a vase and slammed it into his head. The lamp exploded and broken pieces of it rained down on his shoulders. He dropped his other gun as blood ran down the side of his face. He touched it and his fingertips came away bloody. Angrier than he was before, God Body kicked her in the stomach. When she bent over to grab her stomach, he kicked her in the face, knocking her back on her ass.

"You fucking bastard!" LeLe hollered at him, charging at him like a mad bull. God Body whipped his head around, and brought his platinum rosary beads from around his neck. He unsnapped the rosary beads and they appeared as a long as rope, with the beads having been over lapping each other when they hung around his neck. God Body held on to the lower length of the beaded necklace and swung the opposite end of it around in circles, causing it to spin around like a helicopter propeller. Before LeLe could reach him, the godly Crip threw the beaded necklace at her foot. The beaded necklace wrapped around her ankle and he yanked it with both hands. The force from the pull slammed her down on her back and caused her to bump the back of her head. She winced and looked around dizzily.

God Body pulled LeLe in with the beaded necklace and threw the other end of it over the wooden beam of the canopy bed. When he caught the other end of the beaded necklace, he pulled on it with all of his might continuously, until LeLe was dangling upside down before his eyes. He then tied the beaded necklace around the opposite post. He walked over to LeLe, grabbed her by the lower half of her face so her lips would pucker up and kissed her. When he pulled back from her, she spat on the carpeted floor. God Body chuckled evilly and cracked his knuckles. He then started punching her torso like it was a mothafucking Everlast punching bag. Once he stopped he was breathing huskily. He clapped his hands and the music went off. Next, he placed his finger against the ear-bud in his ear and spoke to his guards.

"Y'all niggaz chill out, cuz, I got these two bitchez faded," God Body assured them. "Y'all can fall..."

A sharp whistle from God Body's left stole his attention. He whipped around with a furrowed brow, finding Yada pointing one of his Desert Eagles at him. Her face was twisted in pure hatred; she was clenching her teeth so hard that her jaws twitched.

"Lil' black ass bitch, fuck you plan on doing with that?" God Body went to approach Yada like she was your average bitch, and found out the hard way that she was a mothafucking savage.

Blam, blam, blam, blam, blam!

The impact of the slugs forced God Body back until he went crashing through the floor to ceiling window, hurling towards the ground along with broken glass which twinkled like diamonds under the outside lights. God Body closed his eyes and expelled his last breath while in free-fall. He slammed into the ground awkwardly, snapping the bone in his neck. The rest of him crashed to the lawn, slapping against it lifelessly.

Gun still in hand, Yada ran over to the broken out window and peered down at God Body's lifeless form, confirming his death. She looked at the van she and LeLe had been driven there in and found Voss hopping out of it, holding the driver's door.

"Y'all come on, get the fuck up outta there!" He called out to them and motioned for them to come down. He then pointed his MAC-10 downward and cocked that mothafucka. It was fully loaded and ready now.

Yada ducked back inside of God Body's master bedroom where the guards were still trying to bust through the doors from the opposite side. She shot LeLe down from the beaded necklace and they got dressed quickly. They then tied all the sheets and blankets together to form a homemade rope. They tied one end of it to the post of the bed, and tossed the other length of it out of the broken out window. The lengthy homemade rope nearly touched the lawn below, dangling in place. Carefully yet hastily, the girls made their way down the homemade rope. Once they were halfway down, they jumped down to the surface. As they took off running towards the van, the doors of the mansion flew open. A moment later, the guards ran out with their guns at the ready. When the guards went to fire on Yada and LeLe, Voss upped his MAC-10 and sprayed their asses like cockroaches, cutting them down in a holey, bloody mess. Voss lowered his smoking MAC-10 and pulled open the door of the van, helping the girls inside of the vehicle, one by one. He then slammed the door, and pulled out a small can of lighter fluid.

"Here. Take this," Voss passed Yada his MAC-10. "If anyone comes through those gates, you point it at them, and pull the trigger. You tear they mothafucking ass up. You hear me, babe?"

"I got chu, bae." Yada gripped the MAC-10 with both hands. "What're you gonna do?"

"Y'all probably left some of y'all hairs inside of his bedroom or some DNA somewhere up there. I'ma have to set the bedroom on fire to get rid of any and all evidence." Voss told Yada and she nodded her understanding. Right after, Voss took off running towards the dangling homemade rope. Once he reached the homemade rope, he drenched it with the lighter fluid and set it on fire with his Zippo lighter. Hurriedly, flames ripped up the homemade rope and proceeded inside of the master bedroom, where it engulfed everything else in flames.

Once Voss saw that the fire was doing its job, he ran back to the van and hopped inside. He took off speeding towards the double gates of the mansion, plowing through them and knocking one of them down.

"We did it, we fucking did it!" Voss proclaimed punching the ceiling of the van in excitement, looking back at the girls. They were celebrating like he was hooting and hollering, hugging each other for a job well done. "That's what I'm talking about! My girls were on their shit tonight."

"You were too, baby." Yada leaned upfront and kissed her husband deeply. She then sat back down in the backseat, dapping her homegirl, LeLe, up and giving her mad props. "You was on yo shit, mamas. I'm so proud of you, boo. I couldn't do it without you."

"Thanks, ma, you know I got chu. My mothafucking stomach is killing me, though. That big ass nigga put them mothafucking paws on a bitch, for real for real." LeLe and Yada laughed as she held herself wincing.

Voss could see the pain that LeLe was in and thought it was only right that he blessed her with something for her trouble. "You may be in pain now, but I'm sure that hunnit kay I'ma hit chu off with gon' ease yo suffering, ain't it, lil' mama?" he glanced into the backseat at LeLe.

"Bro, I told you, you were good on this. We're family. I'm just looking out." She tried to assure him.

"I'm just looking out too. That's why wifey getting hit with the same." Voss glanced in the rearview mirror at Yada. She looked like she was about to say something so he continued on. "I don't even wanna hear it. Y'all deserve this paypa I'ma bout to break y'all off. Y'all showed heart, dedication and determination, so it's only right I make sho' y'all straight. You feel me?"

"Girl, we just gon' shut the fuck up and take this fool's money 'cause otherwise we'll be going back and forth all night. You feel me, sis?" Yada dapped LeLe up.

"Yeah, I feel you, girl." LeLe smiled. "Alright, Voss, I'll take my hunnit large in all hunnits, please and thank you."

"Okay, then. That's what I'm talking about. I thought I was gon' have to beat that ass and stuff yo purse with cash. Damn!" Voss chuckled and smiled. And so did the girls. "But for real though. Good looking out, sis." He held up his fist.

"Don't mention it." LeLe touched fists with him.

CHAPTER EIGHT

LeLe kicked it inside of the living room sharing a blunt with Dough Boy and Rampage as they played NBA 2K19. Voss and Yada entered his bedroom, shutting and locking the door behind them. They started kissing, rubbing and touching while peeling one another's clothing off until they were completely nude. Yada took the lead this time, instead of that nigga Voss. She forced him up against the wall with his hands above his head, pinning his wrists down. She then kissed him sensually and thirstily, heavily breathing. Yada sucked on his bottom lip and pulled on it gently, before kissing him once more. Next, she kissed Voss down his chin and licked around his collarbone, tracing his pecks with the tip of her warm, wet tongue. Yada then sucked on his areolas which caused him to shut his eyelids and tilt his head back, gasping. Her sucking on him made his nipples erect and his dick so hard it was standing straight up, pulsating like it had a heartbeat.

"Damn, bae," Voss licked his lips and bit down on his bottom one. "This shit feels good as a mothafucka, on Bloods!"

Yada moved passed his gunshot wound which was still dressed up. She rubbed on his chest and pulled on his nipples, as she softly bit down his abs, heading towards that V that lead towards his hard ass dick. Yada dropped down on her knees and grasped his dick, stroking him up and down. She lifted his dick up and stared up into his eyes, sucking on his smooth nut sack. Voss looked down at Yada as she sucked on his jewels, making 'Mmmmm' sounds. She then put her mouth of his dick and started sucking him off, while tugging on his shit. Her head whipped up and down his shaft, spilling her hot saliva down it. He pressed his hand against the top of her head and guided his dick deeper down his throat, causing her to gag. He would hump her mouth and then push his shit as far as he could down her mouth, then hold it there for a moment. After that he'd continue to hump her mouth, making her gag on his dick again.

"Uh, uh, uh, uh, uh!" Voss said as he stared down into Yada's eyes, mouth fucking her. Having gotten tired of her mouth, he pulled out and directed her to bend over with his finger. He did this while he continuously stroked his dick up and down, making it ooze with its natural nectar. "Now spread yo legs and grab them ankles." She did like he instructed her and shook her ass which made his dick grow harder. Placing one hand on her back, Voss used the other to guide his dick inside of her pussy, feeling her fluffy gushy walls. "Ahh, fuck." He said under his breath, enjoying that wet, hot inferno between her legs. He grabbed her by her hair and pulled her head back. He then used his other hand to grip her meaty hip, slamming his dick in and out of her pussy. His thrusts against her buttocks sounded like masculine hands, clapping hard as fuck. He was beating her shit down, sending ripples up her butt cheeks.

"Faster, harder, ah, ah, ah, ah, ah, ah!" Yada cried out as he fucked the dog shit up out of her. "Smack my ass, baby! Yes, harder, harder! Yes, just like that, just like that!

Smack, smack, smack, smack!

Voss smacked her on his ass over and over again which caused her booty to jiggle while he smashed her out from the back. His face and his entire body glistened because he was covered in beads of sweat from pounding his wife out from behind.

Smack, smack, smack, smack!

"Oh, yes, yes, yes! Keep fucking me, keep fucking me like this!" Yada whined aloud.

"You like this shit? You like how Big Daddy fuck you, huh?" Voss asked, with sweat trickling from the corner of his brow.

"Oh, yeah, I love it!" she swore to him.

When what he suspected having been confirmed, Voss bent both of her arms behind her back and held them down against the small of her back with one hand. Using the other hand, he pulled her hair back like he'd done before, assaulting her rear end with back shots. The sound of masculine clapping hands grew louder and louder, sounding more like gunshots than a round of applause.

Voss was fucking Yada from the back vigorously; sweat rolling down his back, arms and thighs. Yada squeezed her eyelids tighter and licked her lips, feeling his dick pulsating inside of her gooey pussy hole. It was from this that she knew he was about to erupt and spill all of his warm seeds inside of her womb.

"Oh, shiiiit, I'ma 'bouta cum, babe!" Voss shut his eyelids and threw his head back, mouth wide open. He could feel his dick surging with his semen and he was about ready to unleash it deep inside of her pink tunnel.

"Cum in me, daddy! Cum deep inside of yo pussy!" Yada commanded him. Before she knew it, Voss was emptying his nut sack deep down inside of her pussy.

"Uh, Uh, uh, uh, all in this tight mothafucka!" Voss looked down at his dick as he continued to pump her twat. The more he thrust his dick inside of her, the more of his slimy white semen oozed out of her and dripped on the floor. Exhausted and breathing hard, Voss lay back up against the wall, breathing hard. A satisfied and panting Yada, leaned back up against him. She grabbed the back of his neck with one hand and turned her head to kiss him long, deep, and sexually. Voss held her waist as they made out intensely, making 'Mmmmm' and smacking sounds. After they had finished kissing, Yada led him inside of the bathroom where they jumped inside of the tub to shower. They lathered one another up with soap until they were masked white with Dove Soap. Once they rinsed off, they held each other under the spraying showerhead, eyelids closed, mouths shut, enjoying one another's presence.

***

Having placed the last of Yada and LeLe's things inside of the trunk of her car, Voss slammed the trunk shut. He then turned to Yada smacking imaginary dirt from his hands, smiling. "Alright, that's everything." The smile disappeared from Voss's face once he saw teardrops falling from Yada's eyes. "What's wrong, baby?" he approached her, wrapping his arms around her waist. He caressed her cheek with the side of his hand and wiped the tears that kept dripping her grief. "Come on now, lil' mama, tell me what's up? Talk to yo nigga."

"I don't wanna leave you, babe. I really don't." Yada shook her head as she stared into his eyes, a fresh set of tears coating her face. "I wanna stay here with you. Can't I just stay here witchu?"

"I want chu to stay here too, boo, but I need you there keeping up to date on that busta ass nigga's moves. Look, I almost got up what I feel is enough money to go to war with this nigga. Gimme a month tops and I'm at this nigga's throat. I promise, okay?" Yada was looking down and dropping big teardrops, so he tilted her head upwards with his curled finger. Once they locked eyes, she nodded yes. "Gimme a hug and a kiss."

Yada obliged Voss with a kiss and a hug that seemed like it was going to last for an eternity. Once they broke their embrace, they kissed lovingly, and Yada jumped behind the wheel of her car. She threw it in drive and pulled off, wiping the tears from her eyes. She stared into the rearview, adjusting it and watching Voss as he stood in the middle of the street, growing smaller and smaller.

Sitting in the front passenger seat, LeLe wiped the tears dripping from the brims of her eyes. She then reached over and interlocked her fingers with her bestie's, kissing her hand. She stared over at her and caressed her hand affectionately. She hated seeing her so sad.

"Everything is going to be okay, Yada. We just gotta stick with the plan that Voss has to squash punk ass Jabar. Trust and believe in bro, and in no time you'll find yo self reunited with him again. Okay?"

Yada sniffled and nodded, tears steadily dripping from her eyes. She wiped them away with her fingers, but more pooled in her eyes. Seeing this, LeLe popped open the glove box and took out a couple of napkins. She used them to dab away Yada's tears, and then she kissed her on the cheek. Yada looked over at her and smiled. She smiled back, caressing her hand with her thumb as she used her other hand to steer the car with.

***

An all-black van pulled up at the center of a block and its double back doors opened. Two brolic masked up, goon ass niggaz hopped down onto the asphalt. They then reached inside of the van and pulled out a pine box, sitting it down in the street. When they stood back upright they brushed the particles from the pine box from off their hands and looked across the street. They saw three Mexican cats that were in the middle of hustling when they had pulled up. But now they were all headed in their direction, speaking Spanish among one another and toting guns at their sides. The masked up goons' eyes lingered on them for a while before they climbed back inside the back of the van, closing the double doors shut. As soon as the doors were closed, the van drove off, leaving the three Mexicans in the street, staring at its brake lights until it disappeared into the night.

"Who the fuck were those, mayates?" One of the Mexicans said, standing in the middle of the street, gripping his gun.

"I don't know. Probably those Combs faggots." Another one of the Mexicans said.

"Yo, check it out, let's see what's inside the box." The third Mexican said, tucking his gun at the front of his jeans. "Help me open it up, homes." He motioned his comrades over to assist him. They tucked their guns and wedged their fingers into the opening of the pine box's lid and container. They pulled it up as much as they could before the one that had called for help decided to use the butt of his gun to knock the lid upwards, from the wooden container. Once he'd done this, he and his homeboys were able to remove the lid by hand. When they finally uncovered the pine box, they found a muscular man dead inside of it, with half of his head missing.

"Holy shit, it's that foo Maul!" the Mexican that had knocked the lid open with the butt of his gun announced.

"Half of his fucking head is missing, bro." One of the other Mexican's said, looking at Maul's wound wincing. The expression on his face said he knew Maul was in pain from a head-shot like that.

"We've gotta getta hold of Valdez. Shit just got real." The Mexican that had opened the pine box with the butt of his gun said. He tucked his gun and pulled out his cellular, dialing up Valdez.

***

Yada pulled back up to her mansion and jumped out of the car, making her way to the trunk. LeLe had come to stand beside her as she opened the trunk. They had started grabbing their baggage out of the trunk when Jabar's goons had suddenly started appearing out of nowhere.

"Fuck is going on here?" Yada asked them. She'd turned around once she saw them coming her and LeLe's way from the corner of her eye. All of the men had menacing expressions etched across their faces.

Hearing the worry in her bestie's voice, LeLe turned around to see the goons approaching them. One of them tried to grab her and she fired on that fool's grill, busting and bloodying his shit. He stumbled backwards holding his mouth, and two more of them tried to grab her. She tried her best to fight them off, but they'd grabbed her by both of her wrists. One of them wrapped his arms around her body and started carrying her away, kicking and screaming.

"Oh, y'all got me fucked up! You not finna just run off with my bitch!" Yada looked in the compartment where the spare tire was kept and came back up with her .45 automatic handgun, spitting fire at the fuck-niggaz that had snatched up her bestie. One of them caught two in the chest and went down while the other took a headshot, falling to the ground with LeLe in his arms. A distraught LeLe pried his arms from around her and ran over to Yada, getting behind her since she was the one packing the gun that could protect them.

In a domino effect, all those goon ass niggaz that worked for Jabar pulled out their AK-47's and M-4's, pointing them at Yada and LeLe.

"Get behind me," Yada said in a hushed tone to LeLe and pulled her closer behind her. Both of their hearts thudded and they found their palms sweaty when they clenched one another's hands. The girls were afraid. It was showing, but they still were going to show heart.

"What do you think they want?" LeLe asked.

"I don't know, but if we go out then we go out blasting!" Yada swayed her gun around at all the threats surrounding her.

"Give her up!"

Yada and LeLe looked around for where the voice rang from. A moment later, Jabar appeared out of the shadows, walking down the steps of the mansion, calmly. He was unarmed and dressed in all black. His doorag, T-shirt, and Levi's were all black. He was also wearing a big gold cable chain which held onto a medallion the size of a saucer. His name was inside of the medallion in diamonds and set against onyx. Jabar descended the steps spinning the piece casually.

Yada and LeLe exchanged worried glances, then looked back up at Jabar.

"Give up who? And what is all of this about?" Yada asked him.

"I want LeLe's ass." Jabar's face balled up with animosity.

"Me?" LeLe's brows creased with concern. "What did I do?" she inquired from Jabar.

"Bitch you know what the fuck you did, don't play stupid!" spit flew from off Jabar's big ass lips he was so heated.

"I swear to God I don't know, Jabar! Tell me!" LeLe's eyes turned glassy.

Jabar went on to tell LeLe about his belief that she set him up so that Maul could smoke his ass. She shook her head and denied the allegations over and over again.

"If you were in my position, would you believe you right now?" Jabar asked her seriously. LeLe shook her head no. "Good. So you know where the fuck I'm coming from."

"Look, I understand where you're coming from, but I don't wanna die for some shit I didn't do!" LeLe's voice cracked under her emotions and tears trickled from the brims of her eyes. She was emotional and scared. She knew that she and her bestie were at the mercy of their captors' guns, and they could be cut down at any minute.

"That's two fucking bad 'cause I don't believe for one goddamn minute that you didn't have anything to do with setting me up. Shit, I'd be a fucking fool not to believe you weren't involved!" Jabar assured her with fire dancing in his pupils. "Besides, I can't sleep at night knowing only one of you is dead."

"Dead? Oh my God, you killed 'em!" Tears poured from LeLe's eyes as she put her hand over her mouth. She was shocked by the news of Maul's death.

"Don't worry, lil' mama, you gon' be joining that fuck-boy soon." Jabar assured her.

"Over my dead body!" Yada pointed her gun at Jabar. And as soon as she did, the goons pointed their assault rifles at her chest.

"I'm sorry to hear that, sweetness, 'cause I've got big plans for us." Jabar said. He kept on talking seeing that Tankhead was creeping up behind LeLe and Yada, he was creating a diversion for him.

"Ahhhh!" LeLe shrieked as Bang pulled her back from behind and placed his hand over her mouth. He then pulled her arm around her back and put his other arm around her neck, placing her in a choke-hold.

Yada whipped around with her gun up, pointed at Bang, but unable to get a clear shot at him since LeLe was in her way.

"Drop the gun, Yada!" Jabar grumbled.

"Fuck you, Jabar!" Yada called out, with her back to Jabar.

"Sure. Later. But right now I want chu to drop the fucking gun, or so help me, I'll have these goon ass niggaz chop yo pretty ass down in cold blood!" Jabar swore as he clenched his fists.

LeLe locked eyes with Yada and nodded, signaling for her to drop the gun. Yada took a defeated breath and dropped the gun. The metal and plastic handgun clanked once it hit the stoned driveway.

Jabar marched over to LeLe and grabbed her by the hair, pulling her by the hair back towards the mansion. She kicked and screamed, holding onto Jabar's wrist as he dragged her. Still in motion, looking to one of the goons, Jabar whistled at him and he tossed him his AK-47. Bang, the goons and Yada followed them inside of the mansion, through the living room, and down the steps that led inside of the basement.

LeLe lay in a fetal position at the center of the basement floor, crying and holding her aching scalp. Standing over her, Jabar cocked the AK-47 and pointed it down at her. Yada hurried down the staircase and ran over to LeLe, using herself as a human shield.

"No, no, no, Jabar, you can't kill her!" A teary eyed Yada told him as she shook her head, hands up, to show that she wasn't a threat. "She's my sister, my best friend. If you kill her, baby. I know I could never love you! I know we could never be together 'cause I'd never be able to forgive you! So, you think, just think about that before you pull that trigger, okay?" Yada stared into Jabar's face as he thought about the decision he had to make. Her chest jumped up and down as she breathed, fearful, for not only her life, but her bestie's as well.

"Man, fuck that, I say do the bitch! Her hands are as dirty as that mothafucka Maul's is, dawg!" A frowned up Tankhead told Jabar.

"Shut the fuck up, Tankhead. I can't think straight witcho ass steadily talking!" Jabar grumbled at him, then went back to thinking. A minute later he lowered his AK-47 and said, "Okay. I'm not gonna kill her, but she can't stay in Killa Cali. Her ass gotta go. I don't wanna ever see her on home turf again. You got that?"

"Yes. I got it. Thank you." Yada told him and wiped the tears from her dripping eyes.

Jabar handed the AK-47 to one of his men. He then outstretched his hand to Yada and she grabbed it. He pulled her into him, having her so close that she could smell the Kush lingering in his clothes.

"You my bitch now, right?" Jabar asked her, staring into her eyes.

"That's right, I'm yo bitch now, baby. These titties, this pussy and this ass, all belonged to you. My man," Yada claimed, matching his gaze. When she told him what was his, she placed his hands on each body part, and then allowed his hands to rest on her ample ass.

"Good. 'Cause tonight, I want me some of that." Jabar held her gaze as he nodded downward to her pussy.

"Okay." Yada pulled him closer, kissing him deep, hard and lustfully. Pulling back, she sucked on his tongue and then bit gently on his bottom lip. He licked her lips with the tip of his tongue and then kissed her, cupping her big old ass with both of his hands.

"I want chu to take yo girl upstairs and help her pack her shit. I'ma have Tankhead take her to the airport." Jabar informed Yada.

"Where is she gonna go, baby?" Yada looked at him with wonderment written all over her face.

"Where ever she wanna go, but she can't stay here. That's the deal."

Yada nodded and helped LeLe to her feet. She held her hand as she led her upstairs to her bedroom so she could help her pack her things for her flight. Two hours later, Yada was helping a crying LeLe bring her luggage downstairs to the car that Tankhead was waiting for her in. Jabar stood outside on the front porch smoking half of a fat ass blunt, watching as Yada and LeLe stored the baggage inside of the trunk. Once Yada slammed the trunk shut, she turned to LeLe crying, bottom lip trembling. She hugged and rubbed one another's backs, affectionately.

"I'm gonna miss you, girl." LeLe swore with a shaky voice.

"I'm gonna miss you too, Le. Where ever you go, I'll come to visit you every chance I get, okay?" Yada said to her with a shaky voice too.

"I love you."

"I love you too, mamas."

Yada kissed her on the cheek and they hugged again, holding one another for what seemed like an eternity.

"Alright, now, that's enough! It's time for that bitch to go!" Jabar called out to Yada, having just blew smoke out of his nose and mouth.

Yada kissed LeLe one more time before she released her, watching her get inside of Tankhead's car.

As she watched them drive off, tears poured down her face. She wiped them away and waved goodbye to her best friend in the whole wide world. LeLe, still crying, hung halfway out of the passenger window and blew her bestie a kiss, smiling. Yada smiled at her and watched Tankhead's vehicle until it went through the double gates and was swallowed up by the night.

"Come on. It's time to take it in." Jabar dropped what was left of his blunt on the porch and mashed it out underneath his sneaker, leaving a black smear behind. Yada climbed the steps and walked past him, heading back inside of the mansion. He smacked her on her ass and watched her booty jiggle as she disappeared through the doorway.

Tranay Adams

CHAPTER NINE

Jabar wanted Voss dead bad. Although he already had the wolves in the streets looking for the nigga, he knew that they'd really try to find him if he gave them an incentive. And that's exactly what he was going to do. Jabar sent an invitation out to all of the goons of his empire. He knew without a shadow of a doubt that they'd be eager to earn the amount of money he was going to put up for the bounty for Voss.

The meeting took place on a Tuesday night inside of Lyndell's mansion. There were also killaz at the doors and amid the audience to ward off any shit that may occur. They kept these devices on them that looked like handheld vacuum cleaners. They swept this over every nigga that entered the mansion to see if they were wearing any wires. Jabar took the floor, backed by Bang. He kept his finger on the trigger of his M-4 assault rifle as his eyes swept back and forth over the audience. Some of them he knew, while others he was vaguely familiar with.

"First off, I'd like to thank each and every one of you for coming here tonight. Now, on to what I called y'all here for." He cleared his throat and withdrew the sheet from a poster-sized photograph of Voss. "Is every man present here familiar with this bitch ass nigga?" All of the goons in attendance either nodded or said yeah. There wasn't an individual amongst them that didn't know Voss. The nigga had put in mad work for Lyndell's empire. If they hadn't known him personally, then they for sure heard about him on an occasion or two.

Jabar motioned Bang over with a silver brief case. Bang walked over with the briefcase and Jabar popped the locks on it, lifting its lid. There was a total of $100,000 dollars in cold, hard, cash inside. The audience was in awe at the amount of money staring back at them.

"One-hunnit gees." Don Juan started as he looked over the faces of the goons in the audience. "One hunnit racks for the nigga that brings me that cock sucka, Voss's head. Now are y'all tryna get this paypa or what?"

The audience erupted in talks of the bounty on Voss's head. They couldn't help thinking what they could do with that much money. A body was going for twenty to twenty-five grand in the streets, and Jabar wanted them to catch one for one-hundred grand; that was a no brainer. Bang's eyes scanned over all of the goons' faces in attendance and a crooked grin spread across his face. He knew the hardcore killaz were riled up and their trigger fingers were itching now. Every last one of them wanted that one-hundred thousand dollars. Satisfied with their reaction, Jabar shut the briefcase and locked it.

The rest of the night was spent with niggaz eating, drinking and shooting the shit amongst one another. Yada and played the background observing the goons present. She drank whatever they had in her cup and picked over her plate of food. Yada pinched pieces of meat from off her chicken and ate it, watching the men indulge in whatever had them occupied at the time. When she looked to her right, she found Bang approaching her with a plate of food, eating a drumette. He'd just walked away from Jabar who he was chopping it up with whomever about whatever they had on their minds. A smile was stretched across Bang's face as he advanced in her direction, wiping the grease from off his hand with a balled up napkin which was on the side of his plate.

Bang came to stand beside Yada, watching her eat her food for a moment before finally deciding to speak up.

"Soooo, have you thought about what I proposed?" Bang asked her.

"What? You mean, letting you fuck me so you won't tell Jabar that I was the one that broke Voss out of The House of Pain?"

"I'm glad to hear you haven't forgotten. So, what's up? What's it going to be?" he took another bite of his drumette. The chicken he was eating was lemon peppered, which was purchased from Wing Stop. In fact, all of the chicken at the function was purchased from Wing Stop. No one at the gathering like lemon peppered chicken besides Bang, so he had that kind of chicken all to himself.

When Bang posed the question, he and Yada looked up to see Jabar chopping it up with two well-known head bustaz from their organization. He was taking a bottle of Hennessy to the head like it was nothing, and wiping his dripping chin with the back of his hand.

"I'm telling y'all, once we find the traitor that broke Voss outta The House of Pain, and Voss, we hanging their monkey asses up from the ceiling, and going at their asses with an electric saw," he made electric saw noises and pretended to cut into the flesh of the traitor and Voss. The goons smiled and nodded, slapping hands with Jabar.

Having overheard him say this, Bang smiled harder. He figured this would convince Yada to give up the pussy, but, boy was he wrong.

"So, what do ya say, ma?" Bang asked, switching hands with his plate and smacking her on the ass. When he did this, Yada pitched forward and frowned up. She hated when men made her feel like a piece of meat.

As mad as a hornet, Yada turned to Bang and said, "You got me fucked up, nucca! This pussy is not up for negotiation," she smacked the space between her legs which was her coochie. "Fuck you think I am, some kinda cheap thrill? Tell that bitch made ass nigga whatever the fuck you want to? I don't give a fuck!"

Bang looked Yada up and down, hating she wasn't going to go along with letting him smash, but respecting her choice. Still, that wasn't about to stop him from ratting her fine ass out. Nah, he was still going to blow the whistle on that ass.

"Jabar!" Bang called out to his homeboy, stealing his attention from the head bustaz he was talking to. He looked to Bang, still holding the bottle of Hennessy, and threw his head back like *What's up?* "I needa holla at chu, my nigga." He glanced back at Yada to see if she'd change her mind before he walked over to Jabar and spilled his guts. The look she gave him told him that she wasn't going to budge, so he went over to holler at Jabar, taking another bite out of his drumette.

Yada watched Bang closely as he ate his chicken. He wiped his mouth with the balled up napkin before beginning to talk to Jabar.

"My nigga, I know who busted that nigga Voss outta The House of Pain." Bang admitted to him.

Jabar's face frowned up and he stepped closer to Bang. The head bustaz stood on either side of him, waiting to hear the name he would reveal.

"Y—" Bang's eyes bulged and he dropped his piece of chicken. It deflected off the tip of his sneaker and rolled a short distance on the floor. "Ah, fuck, dawg! What the fuck?"

"What the fuck is the matter witchu, nigga?" Jabar placed his hand on Bang's shoulder, looking at him with great concern. At this time, damn near everyone in the party was running over to Bang trying to see what was going on with him.

"Ahhhh, my mothafucking stomach!" Bang's face balled up and he dropped the plate, grabbing his stomach. The plate of food spilled everywhere, and some of the goons stepped on the peas and rice that was on it.

A look of realization came over Bang's face. He looked over in Yada's direction. He found her smiling mischievously at him and eating a piece of chicken. You see, since Yada knew that the lemon pepper chicken wings was the only kind of chicken that Bang loved, and no one else was going to eat them, she poisoned them shits. That way, she didn't have to have his perverted ass to worry about anymore.

Yada continued to smile mischievously and eat her piece of chicken. She sat the piece of chicken down on her plate and waved goodbye to Bang. At that moment, Bang's eyes rolled to their whites. Still holding his stomach, Bang dropped down to his knees and fell face-first into the carpet. Dead!

"Aww, fuck, not my dawg! Not my mothafucking nigga!" Jabar said down on his knees, holding his finger to the pulse in Bang's neck. He was trying to see if he was still alive, but he wasn't. "Who did this shit, huh? Which one of you trifling ass nigga'z killed Bang?" A scowling Jabar looked around at all of the goons.

"I did."

Jabar and his goons looked over their shoulder to where the voice had come from. They found Yada sitting her plate of food down on the mantle and strolled in their direction, continuing to talk.

"I poisoned that mothafucka's food 'cause he tried to blackmail me for some pussy." Yada told Jabar the raw and uncut truth causing everyone in the room to exchange glances.

"Is that, right?" Jabar twisted up his lips like he didn't believe her spiel and folded his arms across his chest. "Fuck he got to blackmail you with?"

"He threatened to tell you that it was me on that tape busting Voss outta The House of Pain, when it was actually his ass."

"Bang was one of the realest niggaz I know. Why in the fuck would he do that?"

"'Cause Voss gave 'em a bag and he believed you wouldn't believe that he did it."

"I still don't believe he did it. I'ma need some kinda proof, sweetheart."

"If you don't believe me, run that nigga Bang's pocket for his car key. Look inside of his trunk. You should see a Nike duffle bag with two-hundred thousand in it. That was the pay-off money."

"Tankhead, look inside of Bang's pocket and get the keys to his Charger. Pop his trunk and get the Nike duffle bag out and bring it in here."

"Alright," Tankhead said, doing as he was instructed. He then ran outside and came back inside of the house with the Nike duffle bag, handing it to Jabar. Jabar walked over to the grand piano, sat the bag down on top of it and unzipped it. He peered inside and saw a shit load of dead presidents. He took out a stack and looked at it, letting the goons see it. A smile spread across Yada's face seeing the money. Truthfully, little mama was the one that had planted it there. She managed to pick pocket Bang during the meeting, load some of her own money inside of an old Nike duffle bag and stash it inside of his trunk. She knew if she was going to go through with killing Bang at the meeting then she was going to need one hell of a reason for it. As well as some proof to go along with her story.

Check mate! Yada thought to herself. She knew that Jabar wouldn't question her story now. Her line of bull-shit was just stamped certified thanks to Tankhead finding the Nike Duffle bag of dead faces.

"Well, your story checks out," Jabar zipped the duffle bag back up and tossed it over to Yada, telling her to keep it. He then turned to Tankhead and pulled out a knot of blue face hundred dollar bills. He peeled off twenty of them and handed them to him. "Take Rondo and wrap Bang's body up. Take 'em down there to Burrell, and have 'em burn 'em at the crematorium."

"Okay." Tankhead stuffed the money inside of his pocket. He and Rondo moved all of the furniture off of the floor-rug and placed Bang's dead body on it, rolling him up tight. They then took the floor-rug out of the house and loaded it into the trunk of his car.

***

"Damn, ma, you gotta big ol' fat ass!" A naked Jabar came behind Yada smacking her on each of her buttocks while stroking his dick up and down lustfully. "Shake that ass for me, ma." Yada shook her ass. She then bounced it up and down, making it clap like a pair of hands. The sight of that big old booty enticed Jabar. He licked his lips and bit down on his bottom lip, continuing to stroke his dick. Jabar loved seeing Yada's thick thighs spread apart, showing her wet, pink tunnel which looked scrumptious set against her dark chocolate complexion. From the look on Yada's face you could tell that she wasn't inside of her bedroom this night, but somewhere else inside of her head. Away from the world and everything that was happening inside of it.

You do any and everything you have to do to keep that nigga'z suspicions to a minimum, even if it means fucking 'em. We're on a mission. And we've gotta do what we've gotta do for our cause. Don't mind we tripping off what chu do with 'em cause after this is all over, we starting over again and we're never gonna talk about this again. You got me? As Jabar slid himself inside of her from the back and started hitting her doggy style, Yada thought back to what Voss had said to her at the hospital. She shut her eyelids and acted like Jabar was killing the pussy. She psyched herself out to believe that Jabar was actually Voss, smashing her from behind.

"Who pussy is this, huh? Tell me who pussy is this?" Jabar said, smacking Yada on either ass cheek, causing ripples to travel up her buttocks.

"Oh, it's yours, daddy! It's yours!" Yada whined like the dick was good, putting on one hell of a performance.

***

Valdez leaned up against the counter watching a young, immigrant Mexican girl whip coke into crack inside of a clear Pyrex pot. Little mama was fresh over the fence of the crime ridden Mexico and could barely speak English. She needed money to take care of her baby, so once she heard from her friend, Alicia, one of the girls she'd illegally entered the United States with, that Valdez' crew was looking for cooks for their organization, she made sure she got her chance to audition for them.

The young Mexican girl, Ruby, father used to work as an enforcer for a cartel over in Mexico until he was murdered for running off with a kilo of coke to feed his habit. When the cartel caught up to him, they executed him and his wife, Ruby's mother, gangland style. Before Ruby's father had gotten murdered he taught her how to cook crack. He used to have her cooking the shit up for him because sometimes he didn't feel like cooking it himself. Anyway, Ruby planned on taking the trade her father had shown her and parlaying it into a paying job...hopefully.

With her latex gloved hand, Ruby motioned for Valdez to take a look inside of the Pyrex pot at the coke she was whipping up for him. "Dese is good, yes?" she asked in her thick ass accent.

"Yes. It's coming along nicely." Valdez smiled and patted her on the back. Right then, his cell phone rung and he looked at its caller identification. Seeing who it was, he motioned one of his goons over to watch Ruby's work while he answered the incoming call. Once the goon had attended to Ruby, Valdez stepped over into the corner of the room and answered the incoming call.

"You've gotta be kidding me, Baby Droopy?" Valdez said in disbelief, rubbing his hand over his bald, tattooed head. "Fuuuck! Ok. Alright. Things are getting rough all over so I'm going to tell 'em to send in the cavalry. No, that was ten guys he sent us, apparently we're going to need more." He disconnected the call and placed another one. As the cell phone rung, he looked over his shoulder to see how Ruby was doing. The goon he'd called over to monitor her was checking out the cookie she'd laid out. When the goon saw he was looking, he grinned and gave him a thumb up, letting him know that little mama could cook. "Yes, hello? Gerardo, I need your help."

***

The raindrops pitter pattered against the passenger window as LeLe stared out of it. Her eyes were pink, and her cheeks had dried tears on them. All she could think about was how much she was going to miss Yada.

She and LeLe had been friends forever. And their parents had known one another for as long as she could remember.

Tankhead glanced back and forth between the windshield and LeLe wondering what she was thinking. He couldn't imagine being in her shoes and having to leave the only place he knew. He was a South Central, Los Angeles native, and he'd been running the streets since before he could piss straight. Dope, coke, crack, weed, meth! You name it; he sold the shit in the streets, getting it how he lived since his parents were too smoked out to raise him.

"Goddamn it!" Tankhead slammed his fist down on the steering wheel. He then pulled over to the side of the road.

Hearing Tankhead cuss up a storm, LeLe's brows furrowed. She looked around wondering where they were going. "What's the matter?"

"Caught a fucking flat, you think you can help me change it?" Tankhead asked her.

"Yeah, sure," LeLe unbuckled her safety belt and hopped out of the car.

Once he hit the hazard lights, Tankhead was jumping out of the car right behind her. He unlocked the trunk and opened it, he grabbed the spare tire out of the compartment it was hidden inside and instructed LeLe to grab the miniature jack. When she bent over inside of the trunk to get the jack like he'd told her, he placed a gun with a silencer attached to its barrel to the back of her skull. Tankhead pulled the trigger and LeLe's brains splattered inside of the trunk, against her luggage. After looking around to make sure no one had seen him lay down his murder game, Tankhead put the rest of LeLe's body inside of the trunk. He then laid the spare tire on top of her and slammed the trunk closed. Next, he ran back over to the driver's side and hopped in behind the wheel, pulling off.

After purchasing a bag of lye and a shovel, Tank-head drove deep into the woods. He dug a six feet deep hole where he tossed LeLe's lifeless body inside. He then covered her body completely in lye, tossed all of her luggage inside with her and buried her. Once he smoothed the dirt out on her grave, he placed the shovel and the empty bag of lye inside of the trunk of his car and drove off.

To Be Continued...
A GANGSTA'S EMPIRE 3

Submission Guideline

Submit the first three chapters of your completed manu-script to ldpsubmissions@gmail.com, subject line: Your book's title. The manuscript must be in a .doc file and sent as an attachment. Document should be in Times New Roman, double spaced and in size 12 font. Also, provide your synopsis and full contact information. If sending multiple submissions, they must each be in a separate email.

Have a story but no way to send it electronically? You can still submit to LDP/Ca$h Presents. Send in the first three chapters, written or typed, of your completed manuscript to:

LDP: Submissions Dept
Po Box 870494
Mesquite, Tx 75187

DO NOT send original manuscript. Must be a dupli-cate.

Provide your synopsis and a cover letter containing your full contact information.

Thanks for considering LDP and Ca$h Presents.

Coming Soon from Lock Down Publications/Ca$h Presents

BOW DOWN TO MY GANGSTA

By **Ca$h**

TORN BETWEEN TWO

By **Coffee**

BLOOD STAINS OF A SHOTTA **III**

By **Jamaica**

STEADY MOBBIN **III**

By **Marcellus Allen**

BLOOD OF A BOSS **V**

By **Askari**

LOYAL TO THE GAME **IV**

LIFE OF SIN II

By **T.J. & Jelissa**

A DOPEBOY'S PRAYER **II**

By **Eddie "Wolf" Lee**

IF LOVING YOU IS WRONG… **III**

LOVE ME EVEN WHEN IT HURTS **II**

By **Jelissa**

TRUE SAVAGE **VII**

By **Chris Green**

BLAST FOR ME **III**

A BRONX TALE III

DUFFLE BAG CARTEL II

By **Ghost**

ADDICTIED TO THE DRAMA **III**

By **Jamila Mathis**

LIPSTICK KILLAH **III**

Mimi

WHAT BAD BITCHES DO **III**

A HUSTLER'S DECEIT 3

KILL ZONE **II**

By **Aryanna**

THE COST OF LOYALTY **II**

By **Kweli**

SHE FELL IN LOVE WITH A REAL ONE **II**

By **Tamara Butler**

RENEGADE BOYS **III**

By **Meesha**

CORRUPTED BY A GANGSTA **IV**

By **Destiny Skai**

A GANGSTER'S CODE **III**

By **J-Blunt**

KING OF NEW YORK IV

RISE TO POWER III

By **T.J. Edwards**

GORILLAS IN THE BAY II

De'Kari

THE STREETS ARE CALLING II

Duquie Wilson

KINGPIN KILLAZ III

Hood Rich

STEADY MOBBIN' **III**

Marcellus Allen

SINS OF A HUSTLA II

ASAD

TRIGGADALE II

Elijah R. Freeman

MARRIED TO A BOSS II

By Destiny Skai & Chris Green

KINGS OF THE GAME II

Playa Ray

By **TJ & Jelissa**

BLOODY COMMAS I & II

SKI MASK CARTEL I II & III

KING OF NEW YORK I II,III

RISE TO POWER I II

By **T.J. Edwards**

IF LOVING HIM IS WRONG…I & II

LOVE ME EVEN WHEN IT HURTS

By **Jelissa**

WHEN THE STREETS CLAP BACK I & II III

By **Jibril Williams**

A DISTINGUISHED THUG STOLE MY HEART I II & III

LOVE SHOULDN'T HURT I II III

RENEGADE BOYS I & II

By **Meesha**

A GANGSTER'S CODE I &, II III

By **J-Blunt**

PUSH IT TO THE LIMIT

By **Bre' Hayes**

BLOOD OF A BOSS **I, II, III & IV**

By **Askari**

THE STREETS BLEED MURDER **I, II & III**

THE HEART OF A GANGSTA I II& III

By **Jerry Jackson**

CUM FOR ME

CUM FOR ME 2

CUM FOR ME 3

CUM FOR ME 4

An **LDP Erotica Collaboration**

BRIDE OF A HUSTLA **I II & II**

THE FETTI GIRLS **I, II& III**

CORRUPTED BY A GANGSTA I, II & III

By **Destiny Skai**

WHEN A GOOD GIRL GOES BAD

By **Adrienne**

A GANGSTER'S REVENGE **I II III & IV**

THE BOSS MAN'S DAUGHTERS

THE BOSS MAN'S DAUGHTERS II

THE BOSSMAN'S DAUGHTERS III

THE BOSSMAN'S DAUGHTERS IV

THE BOSS MAN'S DAUGHTERS **V**

A SAVAGE LOVE **I & II**

BAE BELONGS TO ME

A HUSTLER'S DECEIT I, II, III

WHAT BAD BITCHES DO I, II

By **Aryanna**

A KINGPIN'S AMBITON

A KINGPIN'S AMBITION **II**

I MURDER FOR THE DOUGH

By **Ambitious**

TRUE SAVAGE

TRUE SAVAGE II

TRUE SAVAGE **III**

TRUE SAVAGE **IV**

TRUE SAVAGE **V**

TRUE SAVAGE **VI**

By **Chris Green**

A DOPEBOY'S PRAYER

By **Eddie "Wolf" Lee**

THE KING CARTEL **I, II & III**

By **Frank Gresham**

THESE NIGGAS AIN'T LOYAL **I, II & III**

By **Nikki Tee**

GANGSTA SHYT **I II &III**

By **CATO**

THE ULTIMATE BETRAYAL

By **Phoenix**

BOSS'N UP **I , II & III**

By **Royal Nicole**

I LOVE YOU TO DEATH

By Destiny J

I RIDE FOR MY HITTA

I STILL RIDE FOR MY HITTA

By **Misty Holt**

LOVE & CHASIN' PAPER

By **Qay Crockett**

TO DIE IN VAIN

SINS OF A HUSTLA

By **ASAD**

BROOKLYN HUSTLAZ

By **Boogsy Morina**

BROOKLYN ON LOCK I & II

By **Sonovia**

GANGSTA CITY

By **Teddy Duke**

<u>A DRUG KING AND HIS DIAMOND I & II III</u>

<u>A DOPEMAN'S RICHES</u>

<u>HER MAN, MINE'S TOO I, II</u>

<u>CASH MONEY HO'S</u>

By Nicole Goosby

<u>TRAPHOUSE KING **I II & III**</u>

<u>KINGPIN KILLAZ</u>

By **Hood Rich**

<u>LIPSTICK KILLAH **I, II**</u>

<u>CRIME OF PASSION I & II</u>

By **Mimi**

<u>STEADY MOBBN' **I, II**</u>

By **Marcellus Allen**

<u>WHO SHOT YA **I, II**</u>

Renta

<u>GORILLAZ IN THE BAY</u>

DE'KARI

<u>TRIGGADALE</u>

Elijah R. Freeman

<u>GOD BLESS THE TRAPPERS I, II, III</u>

<u>THESE SCANDALOUS STREETS I, II, III</u>

<u>FEAR MY GANGSTA I, II, III</u>

<u>THESE STREETS DON'T LOVE NOBODY I, II</u>

<u>BURY ME A G I, II, III, IV, V</u>

<u>A GANGSTA'S EMPIRE I, II, III</u>

Tranay Adams

<u>THE STREETS ARE CALLING</u>

Duquie Wilson

MARRIED TO A BOSS…

By Destiny Skai & Chris Green

KINGS OF THE GAME II

Playa Ray

BOOKS BY LDP'S CEO, CA$H

TRUST IN NO MAN

TRUST IN NO MAN 2

TRUST IN NO MAN 3

BONDED BY BLOOD

SHORTY GOT A THUG

THUGS CRY

THUGS CRY 2

THUGS CRY 3

TRUST NO BITCH

TRUST NO BITCH 2

TRUST NO BITCH 3

TIL MY CASKET DROPS

RESTRAINING ORDER

RESTRAINING ORDER 2

IN LOVE WITH A CONVICT

Coming Soon

BONDED BY BLOOD 2

BOW DOWN TO MY GANGSTA

www.ingramcontent.com/pod-product-compliance
Lightning Source LLC
Chambersburg PA
CBHW071127250626
47159CB00006B/2155